The Library
IN EAST AYRSHIRE

H

East Ayrshire
COUNCIL

Please return item by last date shown, or contact library to renew

Louise Pakeman was born in Cannock but has lived in Australia for the past thirty-eight years. Now retired, she has held a variety of jobs including work in publishing, as a freelance journalist and as a breeder of horses and donkeys.

A PINCH OF SUGAR

Eve has always tried to please the men in her life. Then an invitation to spend Christmas in Australia with Bill McMahon, a man she has been corresponding with over the Internet, tempts her to please herself for a change. But her holiday gets off to an unpromising start when she receives a frosty reception from Bill's daughter, Chloe, who knew nothing about her . . . As Eve and Bill struggle to communicate face to face, all appears lost. They must weather misunderstandings and a disagreement before Bill finally realizes what Eve means to him. But is he too late?

LOUISE PAKEMAN

A PINCH OF SUGAR

Complete and Unabridged

ULVERSCROFT
Leicester

First published in Great Britain in 2006 by
Robert Hale Limited
London

First Large Print Edition
published 2007
by arrangement with
Robert Hale Limited
London

British Library CIP Data

Pakeman, Louise, *1936* –
    A pinch of sugar.—Large print ed.—
    Ulverscroft large print series: romance
    1. Single women—Australia—Fiction
    2. Love stories
    3. Large type books
    I. Title
    823.9'2 [F]

    ISBN 978–1–84617–670–8

Published by
F. A. Thorpe (Publishing)
Anstey, Leicestershire

Set by Words & Graphics Ltd.
Anstey, Leicestershire
Printed and bound in Great Britain by
T. J. International Ltd., Padstow, Cornwall

This book is printed on acid-free paper

The secret of living happily with a man
is to take everything he says with a grain
of salt and add a pinch of sugar
to everything you say.

1

Eve rolled half over in the strange bed in which she had zonked out a short while ago; something stopped her going right over. Why was there so little room in a double bed? She reached out a tentative hand and when it touched naked flesh hazily assumed it was her own. Bemused by jet-lag and the drastic climate change from mid-winter to high summer, she hadn't bothered to search for her nightclothes, simply crawled between the sheets without them. The shocking thought that the skin she touched was not her own catapulted her into full consciousness. In one movement she switched on the bedside light, sat up and screamed.

The effect was dramatic. The eyes of the naked man at her side flew open and he stared at her in undisguised horror. Only then did Eve remember her own lack of clothes and endeavour to pull the sheet up in front of herself. She did not succeed because her uninvited bedmate had wrapped it round himself and was clinging on in selfish determination.

As they stared at each other, the bedroom

1

door flew open and the main light went on to reveal a young woman staring at them like some avenging angel.

'Chloe!' the man at her side exclaimed. 'What are you doing? I thought . . . ' His voice trailed away in a mumble in which Eve thought she heard something about *thinking he was in Chloe's bed*. As his words died away, he swung his legs over the side of the bed, remembered his complete lack of clothes and swung them back, endeavouring as he did so to wrap the sheet closer round himself so that more of it was pulled free of Eve's hands.

'Adam! What the hell are you doing?' the young woman in the doorway demanded, her voice shrill.

'N-nothing. I swear — I came to bed — in the room you sent me to. Dropped off my clothes and crawled in without even putting on the light. This . . . woman must have got in after me!' His words had the desired effect of deflecting Chloe's anger; she turned on Eve.

'Just who the hell are you and what are you up to? I don't believe you know my father and I don't know why Steve brought you out here. You conned me into giving you a bed, next thing I know you have lured Adam into it with you.'

'Hey — wait a minute . . . ' Eve started to sit up in bed then remembered she had no clothes on and made another futile attempt to pull the sheet up but her unwelcome bed companion was hanging on to it so tightly it barely covered her nipples. 'Just get this straight — I *do* know your father, he *did* invite me for Christmas. Steve — or whatever his name is — picked me up at the station *at your father's request* and as for this man here, I don't know him from Adam and I haven't the faintest idea why he is in my bed or anything else about him.'

Eve glanced sideways at the man in the bed with her, only to find that he was also taking a peek at her. Briefly their eyes met; embarrassed, they simultaneously turned away. In spite of herself and the compromising situation she had landed in, Eve could not suppress a gasp of disbelief followed by a gulp of amusement when he said in a dry voice, 'Believe it or not, I *am* Adam.'

Chloe nodded agreement and snapped, 'True.' She frowned at Eve and still looked doubtful. Without a word she turned and left the room, returning only seconds later with a man's dressing gown over her arm, which she tossed towards Adam with the single word, 'Out!'

He thrust his arms into the sleeves and

scrambled out of bed, wrapping it hastily round himself. With a rueful look at Eve and what was meant to be a placating one at Chloe, he headed for the door leaving the two women glaring at each other. Eve pulled the dishevelled bedclothes up round her and bit the inside of her lip. She was afraid she was going to succumb to an irresistible desire to laugh. Had she been looking directly at Chloe she might have recognized her own feelings reflected, as her sense of the ridiculous also revived.

'We'll talk in the morning,' Chloe growled. 'Sorry if I jumped to the wrong conclusion,' she added grudgingly, as she closed the door behind her with a firm click.

She directed Adam to the fourth bedroom, little more than a store room but furnished with a divan that looked comfortable enough. When she tossed him a doona and pillow, he guessed this hadn't been her original choice of room for him. Closing the door firmly behind her, Chloe reflected that her handling of the situation maybe lacked finesse. But Dad could have told her that he was expecting a visitor.

'Dad, stop worrying will you? I'll manage,' she had told him when she left him at the hospital. Now the thought crossed her mind that maybe he hadn't been worrying about her at all but trying to find a way to tell her about this person he had apparently invited to share Christmas at the farm. Making soothing noises, she had touched her father's cheek lightly with her lips, abjuring him, as if she were the parent and he the child. 'Now do what you're told and get back home as soon as you can.' She cringed at the memory; he must have felt like hitting her, and probably would have done if he hadn't been so woozy from anaesthesia and painkillers.

'Don't worry about anything, Dad.' Better not to bother him now with the news that she had invited Adam Grant to spend Christmas with them. 'Just mend, I'll cope.'

'Any problems, Steve will help out.' He thought of mentioning that he had already enlisted his neighbour's help but Chloe was moving towards the door.

Chloe's mobile phone rang just as she reached the car.

'I promised your dad you could call on me if you needed help,' Steve told her.

'Thanks, but I am sure I shan't.' Why should both her father and Steve automatically assume she couldn't cope? Farm born and bred and motherless since her early teens, there were few tasks that Chloe could not turn her hand to.

'He has a broken leg,' Steve reminded her,

'so he is likely to be more work than help when he does get home. But I will only be a phone call away.'

Glowing with good intentions bolstered by the knowledge that, barring total disaster, she would not have to ask for Steve's help, Chloe clicked off her phone and headed for home reflecting on the vagaries of men in general.

The message on her mobile had given no indication of when he might arrive, merely that he had been delayed. Had he been more explicit and she less tired and confused by the arrival of a complete stranger on top of her father's accident, the bizarre scene over the bed would not have occurred. She was smiling at the memory as she pulled the sheet up over her shoulders and within seconds fell asleep.

⋆ ⋆ ⋆

Eve tried to get comfortable in the unfamiliar bed but the heat was oppressive. Maybe this was some crazy dream and when she woke it would be at home in England. Life had taken on a dreamlike quality long before the plane touched down at Melbourne and intensified on the train when the ticket collector roused her with a brusque, 'Tickets, please!'

Visiting Australia had been one of those

nebulous dreams carried over from child-hood. Bringing it to fruition the way she had was the unbelievable bit.

The whole amazing sequence of events began when she came across the pen-pal page as she surfed the Net and on a sudden impulse signed on. When the first two correspondents faded out, she was inclined to blame herself for being too dull a person, but the truth was that they did not share enough common interests to maintain a correspon-dence. She was about to give up on the whole idea when she and Bill McMahon made contact. Initially their farming backgrounds kept the emails flying back and forth but soon they found they were sharing ideas on a wide range of subjects from personal details to world politics. When she received a legacy, a pleasing £5,000 from a great aunt she hardly knew, Bill suggested a holiday in Australia. 'Come for Christmas,' he suggested. 'See how you like it here.' Did he, Eve wondered, mean, 'See if we like one another enough to make it permanent'?

On another uncharacteristic impulse she thought, Why not, and bought a ticket before her enthusiasm cooled. Now here she was in a strange bed in a strange country, the only person she knew at all laid up in hospital, lying awake reliving the last twenty-four hours and wishing she could turn the clock back.

She recalled how the warm air, even late in the day, hit her as she stepped from the train at Bendigo. It had surprised her each time after the mid-winter climate she had left behind and she had to remind herself she was now in a different hemisphere. This was the end of the line for the train and she followed the crowds flowing towards the station exit. Everyone seemed to know where they were going or have someone to meet them. Her mind pressed the panic button and she cursed the warm clothing she still wore.

There was no one who remotely resembled Bill McMahon's description of himself among those waiting for the last passengers to leave the station. Just when total panic threatened to engulf her, she heard her own name.

'Eve Manning?' The voice was deep and the twang she caught in those two words was already familiar from the plane. On a deep sigh of sheer relief, Eve opened her eyes and looked up at her rescuer. He fitted her romanticized picture of the Australian male: tall and tanned, casually dressed in denim jeans and elastic-sided boots, topped by an open-necked check shirt. But he was not Bill McMahon, of that she was sure.

'Yes.' She yelped, startled that he knew her name. She breathed deeply. 'I'm Eve Manning,' she acknowledged, relieved that her voice sounded more or less normal. She wanted to ask who he was and how he knew her name but he was already explaining. 'I'm Steve Malone, Bill McMahon's next-door neighbour — he asked me to meet you.'

'Oh,' Eve murmured and waited for him to explain further.

'He is in hospital. But Chloe should be there, time we get home,' he added comfortingly, seeing her look of stupefied horror.

'Chloe?' Eve searched her memory bank but was sure she had never heard the name, certainly not from Bill.

'Bill's daughter.' His tone was terse; anyone who knew Bill well enough to visit should know Chloe was his daughter.

'What is the matter with Bill?' she demanded, remembering that Steve had said he was in hospital.

'He had a bit of an accident . . . ' Steve bent to pick up her largest case, ignoring the wheels and swinging it off the ground as if it only contained feathers.

'An accident?' Eve fell into step beside him as he headed for a somewhat battered and dirty pick-up truck now almost alone in the parking lot. 'What sort of an accident?' she asked, even as part of her brain registered that vehicles like this were called utes here, short for utility vehicle. Bill had explained in one of their emails. '*Aussies always abrieve, it's a hab,*' he had told her.

'Bust his ankle. Slipped off the hay bales on his old truck — he wanted to get haymaking over before you and Chloe arrived.'

The word 'haymaking' invoked for Eve a picture of happy yokels, not trucks of any vintage. 'Sounds nasty,' She commented, feeling even as she spoke that this was a totally inadequate remark.

'Oh, he'll probably be home tomorrow. Bill's a tough old bird but I expect you know that.'

Eve shook her head. 'Not really. I . . . we . . . I . . . ' Her voice trailed away. She could see he was wondering just what she was doing here if she knew so little about Bill.

Steve indicated with a nod of his head that Eve should get in the passenger seat.

As they left the parking area, Eve stole a sideways glance at her companion. She was embarrassed to find him doing the same to her so that for a moment their eyes met. She looked away quickly. Whenever she had thought about her arrival, and God knows she had thought about it often enough, it had never occurred to her that her journey's end would bring her face to face with a total stranger. Stealing another quick glance in his direction she thought with wry humour that she might have caught an earlier train.

The sun had gone down by now but an almost full moon brightened the night and it was still very warm. Eve wished that she had taken off some of her clothes before disembarking from the train, and she also wished she were wearing something more ... well, more attractive. She had been at pains to dress in such a way that she would fit the picture of herself she had painted for Bill. Not exactly dull and stodgy, but comfortable. Not quite middle-aged but getting there, capable, sensible, down to earth. All the things she really was not.

'If it was a bit earlier I would take you round to see Bill — but he will be home tomorrow anyway.'

A reply did not seem called for but she mumbled vaguely to show she had heard.

'Known Bill long, have you?' In spite of the casual voice, Eve knew he was fishing for information, but if he hadn't got it from Bill then she saw no reason to enlighten him.

'Didn't he tell you?' she murmured.

He shook his head. 'Just that you were

coming for Christmas and asked me to meet you.'

'Thank you, I'm glad to be met.'

They seemed to have exhausted communication possibilities. Eve for her part was feeling so spaced out by the change of climate and time zone, which she supposed added up to jet-lag, that intelligent conversation or even coherent thought was beyond her.

Steve's failure to extract any information from his taciturn companion concentrated his physical energies on driving while his mind mulled over the few facts he knew and his imagination supplied those he didn't.

When the vehicle made a sharp turn to the left, Eve was jolted awake sufficiently to register that they were driving between open gates and to observe that the old cream churn doing service as a mail-box bore the legend, 'McMahon' followed by a number, which they had passed before Eve was alert enough to decipher it. As they drew up in a shower of loose gravel in front of what appeared to Eve to be a rambling bungalow with verandas all round, outside sensor lights came on. As Steven switched off the engine the door opened to reveal a young woman peering into the night.

'Aah — here's Chloe!' Eve noted his obvious relief. The sensor lights went out as suddenly as they had come on, leaving the girl framed in a circle of light in the open doorway.

Gathering up her smaller bags, Eve followed Steve up the veranda steps. 'Hi, Chloe, your dad said you would probably be here when I got back from the station with Eve.' He didn't see any need for introductions, assuming that the two women knew all about each other even if they hadn't actually met.

Stepping back to allow Steve in with Eve's case, Chloe looked directly at Eve, who knew immediately their eyes met that she was not expected.

'I thought it was Adam when I heard the car,' Chloe said, making no effort to hide her disappointment. Eve wondered who Adam was and, glancing at Steve, saw he looked as blank as she did.

'Well, I'll be off . . . ' Steve finally broke the uncomfortable silence. Chloe watched him bound down the veranda steps, her mouth slightly open as if she was about to say something. She merely returned his wave as he jumped into the driver's seat.

She waited till the tail-lights disappeared before closing the door and turning to face Eve. For a moment the two women faced one another like wary cats summing each other up.

Eve was the first to speak. 'Look — I'm sorry — it's obvious you aren't expecting me. I — I'll go — find a hotel or something.' She made a half-hearted gesture towards her bags.

'Don't be absurd; you are here now. I probably should know all about you — I must have just forgotten. Anyway, how do you think you can go anywhere at this time of night without a car? Come in — sit down and refresh my memory.'

Eve moved over to the table but remained standing. This situation was worse than anything she had imagined. She took a deep breath and tried to keep the tremor out of her voice. 'Bill asked me for Christmas.'

'Oh — I — see,' Chloe lied. She wondered for a second if Steve had made some crazy mistake; her father had made no mention of a house-guest for Christmas. 'Where have you come from? I mean . . . ' She floundered, realizing this sounded both abrupt and rude. 'Where do you live?' she asked, biting off the question, '*And how the hell do you know my father?*', that trembled on her tongue.

'London.'

'London, England?' Chloe's voice rose in astonishment 'But . . . '

'I got in today; your father told me he

would meet me at Bendigo station. When I got there Steve was there. He said Bill, your father, was in hospital and had asked him to meet me. I — I'm sorry.' Overcome by a wave of sheer exhaustion, she gripped the back of one of the chairs at the table.

Chloe gaped. 'You poor soul!' she exclaimed. 'Sit down before you fall. I'll make a pot of tea. I guess we could both use a cup.'

Eve sat, relieved to find that tea was as welcome a restorative here as at home.

'Why on earth couldn't either Dad or Steve explain about you? But that's men for you,' Chloe grumbled as she filled the electric jug. 'It's a wonder Dad thought to ask Steve to meet you, though I can't think why he didn't ask me. I suppose he has just got into the habit of calling on Steve in emergencies,' she explained. 'He is our next-door neighbour and we always help one another.'

'Do you have many emergencies like this? Strange women turning up out of the blue and needing rescuing?'

'You are the first!' Chloe laughed, placing two mugs of tea on the table. She sat down opposite Eve and, cradling her own mug, asked, 'How did you meet my father?'

'On the Internet.'

'On the Internet?' As Chloe repeated the

words they became an astonished question.

Eve nodded. It sounded so crass. How on earth had she let an unknown stranger persuade her to cross the world? She looked down into her mug of tea, unwilling to meet Chloe's eyes.

'He hasn't got a computer — couldn't work one if he had!'

'If you are correct then I must be at the wrong place entirely.' Eve spoke calmly but her sense of unreality was growing stronger by the minute.

'Well, I thought I was sure, but then I haven't been home at all in twelve months — I suppose he could have learnt. But then surely he would have told me — wouldn't he?'

'Probably not. He didn't tell me he had a daughter or mention me to you so maybe he wouldn't tell you he had a computer.'

'You may be right,' Chloe admitted. 'Though to be fair he didn't know I was coming home for Christmas. I've been teaching away from home. Northern Territory actually. I volunteered to do a year, which was just after last Christmas. I thought he would realize that the year was up and I would be home. I guess neither of us is a very good correspondent. I did suggest to Dad last Christmas that he get a computer and he scoffed at the idea. So I never thought any more about it.'

'Well, apparently he did. He bought a computer early in the New Year, went to classes and took to it like a duck to water, especially the Internet. Said he didn't feel cut off from the rest of the world now. We — he and I — have been talking on the Net for the last eight months or more. I had a bit of a windfall recently and he suggested I come out here for a holiday. Make it Christmas, he said. So here I am!'

'Yeah — here you are!' Chloe was just trying to take in this astonishing information about her father. Her flat tone did nothing to raise Eve's spirits. She must have been mad to hare off across the world at the bidding of a man who hadn't even bothered to tell his daughter she existed. Or tell her the daughter existed. Then to add insult to injury had broken his leg and instead of meeting her as promised vanished into hospital. She was so deflated that she didn't even smile at her own choice of words; in any other circumstances she would have laughed out loud to hear herself use the expression, even in her own mind, about adding insult to injury.

Eve's deep sigh reminded Chloe of her existence and her own obligations. 'I'm sure everything will sort itself out in the morning.

17

It's just that, well, I didn't know anything about you, that's all. I guess I was just feeling a bit miffed that Dad hadn't told me you were coming, just asked Steve to collect you.' She made her sound like a parcel, Eve thought. 'When I heard a vehicle I thought it was the friend I have asked for Christmas. He probably lost himself or changed his mind or something. Don't worry about Dad, he should be home in the morning. They said they only wanted to keep him overnight.'

'You are right.' Eve looked up at Chloe and with a brief flash of optimism managed a smile. 'Things always look better in the morning!'

'You are quite right! You must be zonked. I'll show you to a bedroom, or would you like another cup of tea first?'

Eve shook her head. 'Just bed, I think. It's been some day!' Eve got up and Chloe led the way to a pleasant bedroom; the queen-size bed with the bright quilt turned back smiled a welcome. But Eve was puzzled. 'What a lovely room,' she said, 'but you didn't know I was coming.'

'I told you I was expecting another guest. I expect he will turn up sometime tomorrow.'

Eve was too weary and the bed was too inviting to give any more thought to the person whose room she was taking over.

'Bathroom and all facilities up the hall . . . ' Chloe was saying from the doorway. 'Goodnight — sleep well.'

After the sort of wash her mother had always referred to as a lick and a promise, Eve crawled between the sheets without bothering to find her nightdress. It still felt too warm to warrant it anyway. As the bedside light went out, so did she. Not even someone climbing into the bed roused her.

2

In that pleasant no-man's-land between sleeping and waking, Chloe recalled the events of the previous night. She remembered blundering out of bed and rushing to the guest bedroom to find Adam in bed with the strange Englishwoman. Both were stark naked. With embarrassment she remembered her reaction and knew she had rather lost her cool. With early morning sunlight spreading into the room and the old rooster greeting the new day with familiar arrogance, she could concede that maybe it had all been a genuine mistake, even see the funny side as her sense of the ridiculous asserted itself.

Eve opened her eyes, looked round the unfamiliar room and remembered her dream. By the time she had stretched, yawned and been startled into full wakefulness by her watch telling her it was after 10 a.m., she knew it had been reality. As she snatched up a bundle of clothes and set off in search of a shower, she wondered if Bill's fierce daughter would allow her to stay, even if she wanted to. Feeling more like herself after her shower than she had for a long time, she realized she was also hungry. However embarrassing the situation, she couldn't hide for ever, so she headed for the sound of voices and the kitchen.

Chloe and the man called Adam were at the kitchen table with large mugs of coffee cradled between their hands. They looked up when she came in with identical expressions of rueful embarrassment. Eve smiled and murmured, 'Good morning.'

'Hi!' Chloe greeted her. 'Like some coffee?'

'Please — I would.' Eve realized that she was quite ravenous. She was glad to see that the younger woman's belligerent mood of the night before had dissolved.

'I guess I should say I am sorry,' Chloe said as she put a large mug in front of her and edged sugar and milk across the table. 'I've talked to Dad on the phone; he says he did ask Steve to meet you, and told me about meeting you on the Internet, though why on earth he couldn't have done that before you got here I don't know.' She smiled ruefully across the table at Eve. 'I found a computer in his office.'

Eve thought it was a pity she hadn't thought to look earlier but didn't say so out loud, contenting herself with a nod and a grunt. Not knowing what else to say, she mumbled a vague 'Thanks!' and reached for the cereal packet.

⋆　⋆　⋆

Bill McMahon reflected irritably what a foolish thing it had been to fall off that load and bust his ankle just when Eve was due to arrive from England. He munched the hospital toast and wished to God he had warned Chloe that Eve was coming, or at least told Chloe about her — couldn't think now why he hadn't. It was, he supposed, a childish desire to surprise her with his newly acquired computer literacy that had made him only communicate with her over the telephone or in his usual scribbled longhand letters. As he had met Eve in cyber space, he couldn't really tell Chloe about her without confessing to buying a computer.

He intended to explain about Eve long before she arrived from England, then Chloe called and told him she planned a few days in Sydney on her way back. Even so, if he hadn't been so keen to get the hay in before Christmas and ended up here in hospital, he would still have had time to tell her. He sent up a silent prayer of thanks that Steve had been there or he might still be lying in the paddock.

He knew he would have some explaining to do when he saw his daughter again.

He was right; she had barely installed him in the car, his plastered ankle stretched out on the back seat, before she started.

'Explain, Dad, why didn't you tell me about the computer?'

'I wanted to surprise you. You thought the old dog wasn't up to learning new tricks.' Even to him it sounded weak, and what about Eve? Why hadn't she mentioned her?

'The big surprise was your Internet pen-friend.'

'Aah — Steve collected her, then?'

'Of course he did. Picked her up and delivered her.' Chloe thought that between them they made Eve sound like a parcel. 'How about putting me in the picture, Dad, before we get home?'

'I met her on the Internet. We found we had a lot in common. She told me she had always been interested in Australia, so I said, 'Why don't you come and see it for yourself?', and suggested she make it Christmas. To tell you the truth, I didn't expect her to take me up on it — then she had a bit of a windfall and decided to use it on a trip out here.'

Much the same story as Eve told, Chloe noted, and the woman seemed nice enough, she had to admit. 'As a matter of fact, Dad, I invited someone for Christmas, too,' Chloe said into the silence.

'Oh, another teacher, is she?'

'*He* is a banker.' Chloe stressed the pronoun. 'I met him in Sydney.'

'That's nice.' Bill thought she couldn't have known him long if she had met him when she stopped in Sydney on the way home, but he knew better than to hint at criticism. 'We will be quite a party for Christmas,' was all he said.

'I suppose we are going to the Malones' as usual?' It was a statement rather than a question; they had spent Christmas with their neighbours every year since her mother died.

'Mary mentioned it but I didn't give her a definite answer; waiting to see what you would want to do.'

'Don't put the onus on me, Dad. More likely you were playing for time — you wanted to see what your Internet girlfriend was like before you committed yourself to anything.'

Bill smiled to himself; he had forgotten how perspicacious his daughter was. Ever since she had been knee-high to a grasshopper it had been difficult, if not impossible, to pull the wool over Chloe's eyes.

'Well, perhaps I was,' he admitted. 'Now I'm on crutches maybe we should accept.'

'You could have a point,' Chloe agreed. Spending the day with the large and lively Malone clan might loosen up what she felt could be a difficult house party. 'Yes,' she said now. 'I'll get in touch with Mary and ask her what she would like me to contribute.'

'I wish I wasn't meeting Eve for the first time like this,' Bill grumbled as the car turned up the bumpy track that led to the homestead. 'Go easy here.' He grunted as Chloe showed no sign of moderating her speed in deference to his injury.

'Hi — we're back!' she called hopefully, drawing up below the veranda and getting out to help her father clamber awkwardly from the car and take a couple of difficult steps towards the house. There were no hurrying footsteps or outstretched hands to help her assist him into the house.

'No answer — came the stern reply,' Bill muttered as he dropped heavily into a chair. In spite of herself Chloe smiled. This was one of her father's favourite sayings and as a small child she had argued with him, pointing out that if there was no answer then there wasn't a reply — stern or otherwise.

'Great welcoming committee,' he muttered. 'I could do with a cuppa,' he added hopefully.

But Chloe had moved over to the window where she saw two figures, apparently deep in conversation, walking towards the house. As she watched they both laughed; the thought that they were probably recalling their unorthodox introduction annoyed her.

But it was their names causing the hilarity.

'Is your name really Adam?' Eve asked.

'And are you truly Eve?' He was having difficulty accepting such a coincidence.

'Our visitors are on their way to the house.' Chloe half-turned to her father. 'But they don't seem to be hurrying.'

Bill shifted in his chair and banged one of his crutches on the ground without knowing he had done it; it was an expression of his frustration and annoyance that he couldn't leap to his feet and cross the room to take a look at this woman he had invited to visit from the other side of the world. Chloe moved away from the window, still scowling, and switched on the electric jug.

Bill stared at the woman who came through the door; she didn't look at all middle-aged and certainly not like a grand-mother. She was slim, and very attractive, and nearer in age to the man with her than to himself. He cursed the plaster that stopped him crossing the room to greet her. At forty-five and temporarily crippled, he felt old.

He glanced at Chloe's unsmiling face, felt a

tightening in the atmosphere without quite understanding it and wished he had never issued his impulsive invitation. The prospect of a merry Christmas faded. Then the woman — for one panic-stricken moment he forgot her name, crossed the room, hand extended.

'Hello.' He noticed the pleasant soft tone of her voice, and found he was smiling as he reached for her hand.

'Hello, Eve.' Her handshake was warm and firm; he liked that. 'Welcome to Australia. Sorry I couldn't meet you . . . but . . . ' Bill nodded towards his plaster. 'I hope you had a good journey?' Eve warmed to the tone in his voice, he sounded as if he really cared.

'Yes, thanks.' She smiled. 'Nothing untoward happened and we arrived on time.'

'I should have met you at the airport.' If only he had, Bill thought, he might not be nursing a broken ankle now.

'I'm sorry about your ankle. Rotten luck just before Christmas,' Eve murmured sympathetically, and he wondered if she had read his thoughts.

'If I am honest, I must admit that it was carelessness rather than bad luck, and now there seems nothing to do but grin and bear it.'

'Yes . . . ' Eve murmured, wondering even as she said it if that were the required response. When he didn't speak and the silence between them quivered with unspoken words, she reflected that meeting in person was much more complicated than chatting in cyber space. When they spoke it was in unison.

'I suppose — ' Bill began.

'It seems — ' Eve said. They stopped as they had begun, together.

'Ladies first,' Bill invited gallantly.

'It seems strange to be here in high summer with Christmas so close.'

'I was about to say the same.' Bill smiled. 'It must seem odd to you, celebrating Christmas in summer. I have heard other English people say that. Maybe we should have two Christmases, one in June for you folks and one in December for us home-grown Aussies.'

Eve smiled. 'Sounds like a good idea — two for the price of one. I've heard that Australians are always ready to party.'

'That makes us sound a very frivolous nation.'

'Oh, I didn't mean it as criticism — quite the reverse, in fact.' Eve hoped she wasn't going to put her foot in it every time she opened her mouth and told herself that if Bill seemed touchy it was understandable. In his place she would be downright grouchy. 'Is it

— painful?' she asked, nodding her head in the direction of the plaster cast.

'Not so bad — now. Cumbersome and a damn nuisance.' He sighed, and banged the ground irritably with one of his crutches. 'God knows how long it will take me to master these wretched things.'

'Not long. I broke my ankle once and thought the same but to my surprise I was hopping about on one leg almost as fast as I could move on two in no time.'

'I expect you were a lot younger than I am.' His tone said he didn't believe her.

'Well, yes, I was at school,' she admitted. 'It would probably take me a bit longer now.'

Bill grunted, unsure how to answer. To agree with her might be taken as a suggestion that, like him, she was about to tip over the hill, something he could see was far from the truth. In fact, he was somewhat dismayed at her youthful appearance. Learning from their Internet correspondence that she had recently become a grandmother, he had expected someone more, well, grandmotherly than this attractive woman barely dipping into middle age.

His invitation had been so casual that he was barely aware he had issued it until she surprised him by accepting. Eve, sitting by him was just as surprised to find herself so far from home with Christmas around the corner. The strangeness of everything made her feel oddly detached and at the same time pierced by a totally unexpected shaft of longing for the familiar. Maybe it was still the effect of her sudden transition from one hemisphere to the other, one time zone to its opposite, from mid-winter to mid-summer. She supposed this was what they called jet-lag, this feeling of disconnection from her surroundings and the people she was with, even from herself. She had tried to convince herself that last night had been nothing more than a bizarre dream. Then out there with Adam she had to accept that, embarrassing as it was, it was not. 'Sorry?' She emerged from her thoughts to realize that Bill was speaking. 'You've met Adam then?'

'Yes — yes, I — er met him . . . ' She trailed off, hoping he would not question her about the meeting and asked a question of her own. 'Has Chloe known him long?'

Bill shrugged. 'I wouldn't know. I didn't know he existed until she told me she had invited a friend for Christmas. I assumed it was one of her girlfriends — stupid of me.'

'She seemed, well, surprised when I arrived.' Eve suppressed her irritation; after all, he had failed to tell Chloe he had invited her. 'It seems neither of you mentioned the fact that you had invited a guest for Christmas.' Perhaps this was an extreme example of laissez-faire?

Detecting the censure, Bill bit off a sharp retort. There was no point in quarrelling so early in what could well be a difficult visit. 'We like to think we have an open house for everyone.'

Neat, Eve thought. She couldn't argue with that.

'What do you think of him?' Bill asked after a silence lasting so long that Eve almost lost the thread of the conversation.

'Who?' she asked vaguely. 'Oh, Chloe's friend?'

Bill nodded.

'I've barely met him.' An apt statement. 'But what I have seen of him, he seems very nice.' What an understatement. What she had seen of him — in her bed — had looked better than 'very nice'.

'Hmmm. And what about Steven — the one who met you last night?'

'Very nice too,' Eve answered cautiously and diplomatically. Was she to be questioned on every man she spoke to?

'I always hoped that Steven and Chloe would make a go of things. They were great mates as kids. I thought . . . ' His voice faded out and his slight frown was replaced with a somewhat forced smile as Adam appeared.

'G'day, Mr McMahon — nice property you have here.' He looked round appreciatively. 'How's the leg today?'

'Feeling somewhat better, thanks! But the rest of me feels mad with myself for doing such a damn-fool thing right on Christmas.' He nodded at the crutches propped up at his side. 'I suppose I will get the hang of those things one day — probably the day I don't need them any more.' He gave a wry smile.

'Oh, you will be skipping around like a two-year-old long before that. As for doing it at Christmas — well, that is probably good, not bad, timing. Plenty of folks to give you a hand.' Adam's voice was deliberately cheerful.

Bill, unconvinced, had the feeling that such vague cheeriness might well be all Adam had to offer.

'You live in Sydney?' Eve broke the silence in a voice that, to her own ears at least, seemed over-bright.

Adam nodded. 'Yes.'

Eve gave up and murmured, 'I wonder if Chloe needs any help,' and left the two men alone to carry on the conversation — or not — as they pleased.

'Hi! Anything I can do to help?'

'You could dry up.' Chloe felt slightly ashamed at the ungracious note in her voice.

Eve was, after all, a visitor to Australia as well as to their home. The unfortunate incident of the previous night had not been her fault — if she was honest, she herself had been as much to blame as anyone. Annoyed with Adam for arriving so late, she had possibly been vague about where he was to sleep. It was only when she didn't hear him making his way to the room near her own that she thought she had better see what had happened to him. Unable to locate him, she had cautiously opened the door of the guest bedroom, the one she had originally planned for him, and was galvanized into shocked alertness to find him asleep *with* their other guest. She dismissed, almost before it formed, the thought that she would have preferred him to be in *her* bed. In the cold light of day, she was beginning to see the humorous side, and to feel a trifle sorry for Eve. She considered her now as someone in her own right rather than an unexpected and, she had to admit, unwanted guest, and saw a pleasant enough woman no longer young yet barely middle-aged offering help. Hardly a man-eating siren, she was probably genuinely shocked to wake up and find Adam beside her.

Eve realized that Chloe's acceptance of her

offer of help was an overture and tried to make light conversation as she dried the dishes.

'I shall have to go shopping tomorrow — it is Christmas Eve and the fridge and pantry are just about bare. Want to come with me?' asked Chloe.

'Oh yes, please, I would enjoy that, but — '

'Oh, don't worry about Dad.' Chloe guessed that Eve was thinking about Bill. 'He will be fine. I just have to shop or we will all starve to death. We have been asked to the Malones' for Christmas Day — they are our neighbours. Steve, who met you, lives with his parents, but they are a big family and most of them will be there. You'll like them,' she assured Eve, after a pause to take a deep breath.

'I look forward to it.' Eve tried not to sound doubtful. Inwardly she quailed at the prospect of facing up to a large gathering of strangers and being presented as — what? Bill's English girlfriend? She hoped not.

'I want to be off in good time, it will be such a scrum; everybody doing last-minute Christmas shopping. Can you be ready by 8.30?' Chloe asked.

Eve assured her she could and by 8.20 the following day she was watching Chloe gather up car keys, purse and calico shopping bags.

'Glad to see Dad is environmentally aware.' She grinned. 'We're off to the shops!' she called to the men. 'Eat what you can find.'

Eve, with a quick 'Goodbye!', hurried after Chloe; Adam half-rose from his seat as if he would follow them, then dropped back and turned to Bill. Eve, hurrying out in Chloe's wake, did not hear what he said. She smiled to herself, enjoying the crisp brightness of the early morning and a sudden sense of freedom. When Chloe turned to her with a smile as she settled in the passenger seat and confided, 'It is good to be off on our own,' she knew the feeling was mutual.

'Dad is like a bear with a sore head — all shitty because I hadn't told him Adam was coming,' Chloe complained as she started the car. 'But he — '

'Didn't tell you about me.' Eve supplied the missing words when Chloe stopped abruptly. 'Your father has a very sore leg,' she felt bound to point out.

After a short silence in which Chloe grappled with her thoughts, she half-turned to Eve. 'It was a bit rough on you, I realize, crossing the world only to find no one seemed to be expecting you.' Eve recognized this as the olive branch it was intended to be.

'Past history. Tell me where we are going,

what we are going to do, all about Christmas in Australia.'

'We-e-ll — today we are going up the street — '

'Before you go any further,' Eve broke in, 'maybe I need a crash course in Australian idioms.' She looked round at the countryside. 'For instance, what do you mean by *up the street?*'

'Into town, to shop,' Chloe explained. 'I suppose referring to the street does sound odd when we are out here in the bush — '

'Bush?' Eve interrupted.

'Countryside, as distinct from suburbia or city,' Chloe explained.

Eve nodded. 'So we are leaving the bush and heading up the street and that, in plain English, means we are going into town to shop?'

'Right!' Chloe grinned. 'But out here we are the ones speaking plain English.'

Eve smiled back, deciding that she liked her companion very much in spite of the inauspicious start to their relationship, and it would be fun learning Australian and all about this fascinating upside-down country where Christmas came in mid-summer.

As they drove into the town, Eve caught sight of Santa, with beard and red suit with faux fur trim. The day had warmed up

36

considerably since they left home and she felt a surge of sympathy for him, tinged with amusement at the incongruity of the large shades he wore. She noticed some shops had decorated their windows with fake snow scenes; this struck her as being faintly absurd, with the temperature nudging thirty. As if she had picked up her thoughts, Chloe gestured contemptuously at one of them. 'It's time we acknowledged that Christmas is a summer festival and stopped copying the northern hemisphere.'

'And let poor old Santa wear shorts?' Eve suggested with a grin.

'Exactly!'

They had been climbing slightly as they drove through the city and Chloe turned into a large car park that serviced a shopping mall much as Eve was used to at home. 'I'm heading for Safeways,' Chloe explained. 'I hope you don't mind shopping for groceries but we can get just about everything there. It's such a bind finding parking if we go from shop to shop. From the look of the fridge, Dad hasn't had a decent shop for ages.'

'Do you have parking problems here too?' Eve was surprised, it didn't fit in with her inner picture of a great empty land.

'We've got unlimited space in the centre of the continent but it's the outside where the

37

population is; Bendigo is growing fast but parking spaces diminish at the same rate. Here you can usually find a spot, without parking fees.'

Chloe seemed to be stocking up for a siege, Eve thought, as she followed her round the supermarket. The piped music churning out a stream of Christmas songs and carols seemed at odds with shoppers dressed in summer clothes and pushing trolleys loaded with fruits and salads and great slabs of pink watermelon.

'Do you have a traditional Christmas dinner?' Eve asked on the way home.

'Depends what you call traditional. If you mean roast turkey, hot veggies and Christmas pudding, well, some still stick to the English menu but a lot of people now are coming to their senses and opting for something more suitable for Christmas in mid-summer. I guess the women are responsible for that. I can remember my mum getting up with the rooster's first crow to start the turkey roasting. By the time we actually sat down to the meal, the temperature was often thirty plus outside and about sixty inside with the old wood stove going full blast and no air-conditioning. After all that effort, no one felt like eating.'

Eve felt a rush of sympathy for Chloe's

mother. 'What do most people have nowadays?'

Chloe half-turned with a lop-sided smile. 'You are wondering what sort of lunch we will get at the Malones' tomorrow?'

'Well, yes . . . ' Eve admitted. 'I suppose so.'

'You can look forward to a genuine Aussie Christmas: cold buffet, barbecue for those who feel deprived without hot meat, frozen Christmas pudding, fruit salads, pavlovas and of course mince tarts.'

This sounded more than acceptable to Eve, although she did wonder aloud, 'Frozen Christmas pudding?'

'Dried fruits in ice cream. Very nice, very rich and probably very fattening.'

'Sounds good,' Eve said as she got out of the car to help Chloe with the shopping. Working as a team, Eve carrying and Chloe putting away, they soon had the car empty and the fridge full. Still working companionably, they put bread, cheese, salads and fruit on the table for a simple lunch.

'Are you planning to go to midnight mass?' Bill asked Chloe.

She stared at him for a moment, coffee pot aloft. 'Are you?' she shot back.

'Hobble up the steps into the cathedral on these?' He kicked the crutches propped against his chair with his good foot.

'You haven't been to mass — midnight or any other — for years.' Chloe dismissed the idea with a shrug and continued to pour coffee.

'Well, I would have gone tonight — to show Eve our cathedral.' He smiled across the table at her, glanced briefly at Adam and added, 'Adam, too.'

'Would you like to go?' Chloe asked. 'Either or both of you? It is quite a tourist attraction, actually.' She felt constrained to add, 'The largest Gothic cathedral in the southern hemisphere. It looks its best for midnight mass, inside and out.'

Eve was glad she had accepted Chloe's offer when she stepped out of the car shortly before midnight and looked with awe down towards the panoramic building lit up below her. As she followed Chloe and Adam up the stone steps, a breeze, warm and featherlight, touched the bare skin of her arms, making it even harder to take in that this was Christmas. The moment had an air of unreality and, like everything and everyone she had encountered so far in Australia, was nothing like her preconceived ideas.

3

Eve woke to bright sunshine pouring into her room on Christmas morning. She remembered the sun setting in a crimson sky the night before and smiled when Bill quoted the old saying 'Red skies at night, shepherds' delight. It was a great sunset last night.'

'I have always heard it as sailors' delight.'

'I'm a farmer,' Bill pointed out to Adam.

'My father said the same as you,' Eve told Bill. 'He was a farmer too.' She sensed the tension bordering on dislike between the two men.

Bill, with a triumphant glance at Adam, said, 'There you are. Even on the other side of the world they say shepherds.'

Eve glanced at Chloe and their smiles conveyed their feeling that men could be very childish. With a shrug Chloe began to fill the baskets and car coolers standing on the kitchen table with vast quantities of food.

'Are we going to need all this?' Eve was astonished at the quantity.

'Probably not, but anything that doesn't get eaten can come back. Think how it is going to save cooking over the next few days!'

Eve had to admit that was good sense.

'I want to make sure that Blossom and her calf are separated before we go.' Chloe turned to Adam. 'Coming?'

'Sure.' He pushed back his chair. 'So long as you don't expect me to milk a cow or anything.'

Adam looked doubtful, but Eve broke in eagerly, 'I wonder if I can still milk. I haven't tried for years.'

'It's like riding a bike,' Bill said from the doorway. 'One of those skills you never forget.' He made his way with some difficulty over to the table and dropped into a chair. 'Put some toast on for me, will you, love?' he said to his daughter. 'I'll give cereal a miss while we've only got that watery bought stuff to put on it.' He indicated the bottle of milk. 'I guess none of us needs a great breakfast anyway with one of Mary Malone's Christmas feasts ahead.'

Eve, who was nearest the toaster, quickly dropped a couple of slices in. Chloe smiled her thanks and continued on her way out, with Adam behind her.

'How do you like your tea?' Eve asked as she pulled a mug forward. 'Milk, sugar?'

Bill nodded. 'Not so much of the first, plenty of the latter; hot, strong and sweet.' He paused before adding with a grin, 'Like love.'

'You sound as if you are feeling somewhat better this morning.' She smiled, pushing the steaming mug towards him.

Bill returned her smile. 'Thanks! How come you know how to milk a cow?'

'I was brought up on a farm.'

'Ah, yes — I was forgetting. I know your husband had a manufacturing business.'

'A shoe factory. But my father had a farm, well, a smallholding, really; he had been a herdsman on a big estate before he married and got his own place, and what he had always wanted, his own Jersey herd.' She smiled reminiscently. 'I was brought up in the belief that the stuff in a bottle had nothing to do with cows.'

'I reckon your father and me would get along fine if that is what he taught you.'

'Yes,' Eve agreed, as memories of her childhood swept back. 'I think you would.'

In the silence that followed, Eve reflected that it had been easier to talk through a computer than face to face.

Bill concentrated on spreading his toast with honey that was crystalized to the point where it was virtually impossible to spread without reducing the toast to a pile of sticky crumbs. He had just taken a large bite of toast and honey — or honey and toast, for the bite he had just bitten off was primarily a large lump of solid honey — when the door was flung open and Adam, liberally doused in cow manure, burst in.

'What in the world — ' Eve began, then caught the glint of sardonic amusement in Bill's eyes and before she could stop herself a bubble of laughter escaped and developed into a helpless giggle.

'For God's sake, get out of those clothes and into the shower!' Chloe sounded anything but sympathetic as she appeared in the doorway behind him. 'You are dripping all over the place and you are not very sweet on the nose either.'

'Oh, thanks a lot — I came out to help you and this is what I get!'

'Not from me you didn't.'

Eve's strong sense of the absurd came to the fore. 'I should hope not!' Bill guffawed in appreciation.

'Very funny indeed!' Adam lost his cool along with his dignity.

'No, of course it isn't . . . ' With a supreme effort, Chloe kept both her voice and face expressionless. 'Just get into a hot shower with your clothes — that will get the worst off them — then bring them out here to the washing machine. Go on!' she urged as Adam remained where he was, the picture of helpless misery. Thus goaded, he headed for the bathroom. Chloe sighed. 'Oh dear, what a mess.' As she was looking at the floor as she spoke, Eve wasn't too sure where her real concern lay — with Adam or the mess to be cleared up. 'And I still haven't got that damned awkward old Blossom separated from her calf. Perhaps Steve will help me when he gets here.'

'I'll help you,' Eve volunteered. 'I know enough about cows to keep a reasonable distance from the messy end.'

Eve had experienced what to many would be a tough childhood — both parents had little time for much but work and Eve was expected to do her share as soon as she could toddle. It had been her father's proud boast that his three-year-old daughter could milk a cow. In spite of, or because of, this the young Eve dreamed of becoming a schoolteacher. But ambition and hard work stood her in little stead when her mother died. Her father saw no valid reason to keep her in school when he needed her at home. So at sixteen she folded her dreams away and did her best to take her mother's place in the kitchen and the dairy. Eve knew about cows. 'Sorry — what did you say?' Eve came back to the present with a start as she realized that Chloe was speaking to her.

'I don't want her going out there. Grab that

stick and stop her, will you?'

Blossom, shocked to see a total stranger blocking her way, did not argue the point.

Chloe heaved a sigh of relief. 'Thanks. Believe it or not that was all I wanted Adam to do but before we got to that stage he had managed to stand right behind her and cop the lot!' Eve returned her smile with one that acknowledged the sisterhood of women and the ineptitude of men.

'I should have done this yesterday,' Chloe admitted. 'We will have milk over the holiday period, but I would have liked some cream for today. Dad only milks her a couple of times a week; the rest of the time he leaves the calf with her. That's why she is a bit difficult — she doesn't have a regular routine.'

'Cows, like most animals, are sticklers for routine.' Eve remembered her father's Jerseys lining up at the gate at milking time.

'Not much of a country boy, your young man,' Bill commented dryly as they walked in. 'He hasn't finished cleaning himself up yet. Hope he realizes all our water comes out of the sky.'

'Don't grouch, Dad.' Chloe remonstrated. 'He has to get clean — he can hardly go to the Malones' looking and smelling like that. And just for the record, he is not my young man. And cows, or water from rainwater tanks, are not part of his scene; he is not, as you observed, a country boy.'

'OK, OK.' Bill spoke in a would-be soothing voice and put out a hand as if to smooth his daughter's ruffled feathers.

'Well, one doesn't meet many cows in city banks, Dad, he works in Sydney.'

'How did you meet him?'

'At a party — I was taken along by a friend and so was he. Turned out we were the only people there who hardly knew anyone else so . . . ' She shrugged, indicating that the rest was self-evident. 'We met again and when I realized he had nowhere to go for Christmas . . . ' Her voice faded out as she heard the bathroom door.

'Steve will be here in a minute.' She glanced at her watch. 'I guess I'd better be ready. She looked down ruefully at the old jeans and shirt she had worn to do the chores. 'I can hardly go like this — not on Christmas Day, anyway! Where did Eve go?'

'She followed me into the bathroom.' Adam, looking, smelling and feeling more like himself, came into the kitchen.

Chloe frowned slightly; Eve had looked fine to her. 'Hope she won't be long. I need to shower.'

Steve came in from the yard just as Chloe

joined the others. She looked cool and fresh in a rose-pink shift, her bare feet in sandals and her short hair still damp from the shower. He thought she looked enchanting and his warm smile embraced her before taking in the others. 'Merry Christmas, everyone!' He beamed. 'I've borrowed Dad's station wagon,' he told Bill. 'You can stretch your leg along the back seat and I can load food in the back. There is a cargo barrier so it won't land in your lap.' He turned to Adam. 'You can come with me and the girls can follow in Chloe's car.'

Eve thought that quite an acceptable arrangement but Adam looked mulish. 'I'll go with Chloe.'

'Well, come on, then, help me carry some of this stuff.' Chloe's brisk tone fell just short of snappy.

Eve turned to Bill, ready to help him down the veranda, but Steve had already offered his arm.

Eve followed, feeling a bit like a parcel that everyone had forgotten. By the time Bill, his crutches and his plastered ankle were settled in the back seat of Steve's station wagon, Chloe had already left in her small two-door saloon, so Eve climbed into the passenger seat beside Steve.

'We could quite easily have got your father,

his girlfriend and all this stuff to wherever it is we are going, without help.' Adam hadn't taken to Steve and he would have welcomed the chance to be genuinely useful after the fiasco with the cow.

'I guess he needed to help. He blames himself for Dad's accident as he was with him.' They drove in silence for a few minutes then Chloe steeled herself to offer Adam the apology she knew was overdue. 'I'm truly sorry about the night you arrived. I shouldn't have yelled. It must have been scary for you as well as Eve.'

'Oh, I just thought it was an example of local hospitality.'

Catching the amusement beneath the serious voice, Chloe emitted a small chuckle when he added, 'Your English visitor probably thought that too.'

The doors of the Malone home were open and as the two cars drew up people spilled out on a wave of party noise, willing hands eager to help Bill. Eve following with her arms full of food was quickly swept up in the general welcome.

Chloe called cheerfully, 'Happy Christmas, everyone. Let me introduce our guests — Adam from Sydney and Eve from England.'

'The Cosmic Joker at work again!' Steve

commented into the hiatus as the chorus of 'Hi' and 'Merry Christmas' died down.

'Steve's little joke,' Chloe explained. 'He always says it is the work of the Cosmic Joker when something odd or coincidental happens.'

'I see,' Eve murmured politely, not sure she did and hoping this Adam and Eve business was not going to haunt her for the duration of her stay in Australia.

'Hello, Chloe. I'm Mary Malone, and this — ' She waved a hand vaguely in the direction of the noisy crowd ' — is my family. Well, most of them are, anyway.' Eve found herself claimed by an attractive woman about ten years older than herself. 'Come and meet my husband. Last time I saw him he was settling Bill in a comfortable spot on the veranda. No doubt putting the world to rights, or farming.'

They found the two men discussing haymaking.

A soft sigh escaped Eve as she sat down by Bill. Interpreting it correctly he smiled at her. 'The Malones are lovely people but a bit overwhelming en masse.'

'Yes,' Eve agreed, 'I hadn't expected there to be quite so many. Do you think I will ever sort them out?'

'Steve, you already know, Mary has

introduced herself and that was his father, Mick, I was talking to. Steve has three sisters, two married and with kids, those two guys over there are their husbands and the old lady in the rocker is Grandma, Mary's mum. The only person not actually family is Gary Talbot — he farms on the other side of Malone's place. He and Steve have been mates since before primary school.'

'I can't say I have everyone tagged but I'll work on it,' Eve promised with a smile. 'You look . . . ' She had been about to say 'more like yourself' then realized she didn't really know what that was, so substituted a simple 'better'.

'I feel it, or maybe just getting used to this.' He nodded at the plaster cast. 'But I feel mad with myself for letting this happen just before your arrival. A week earlier and I could have asked you to put off your visit for a couple of months.'

'I'm glad you didn't,' Eve said with genuine conviction. 'I'm really enjoying myself.' It was true, and what she was enjoying as much as anything was sitting with Bill and watching the people partying round her.

Adam was keeping close to Chloe but she was watching Steve's pretty younger sister moving out on to the veranda with Gary Talbot. Eve noted that when Chloe turned back to Adam her smile was a little too bright and did not reach her eyes. When Steve also moved out on to the veranda, she was surprised to see him jump down the steps and half-run in the direction of the farm sheds.

'Steve is checking Etty,' Bill told her, answering her unspoken question. 'He thinks she might foal today.'

'Etty in foal?' Chloe, on her way out to the veranda with Adam, both with plates of food, stopped in front of them. 'Neither of you told me.' She looked down at the laden plate in her hand as if surprised to see it there. 'Here, Dad — I brought you some food.' She said impulsively, 'And Adam brought you some, Eve.'

From the expression on Adam's face, Eve knew that the loaded plates had not been destined for either Bill or herself, but she accepted the one being surrendered to her, suppressed her amusement and thanked Adam.

'Enjoy!' Bill raised his fork in a mock salute, adding in a dry voice as he watched Adam trail after his daughter, 'I hope that young man puts up a better show when presented with a foaling mare than he did when asked to help with the cow.'

'Me too.' Eve grinned at Bill and they

shared a moment of wry amusement. She was about to add that Christmas seemed an odd time for a foal to be born then remembered that it was mid-summer here, not mid-winter.

'Is she a valuable horse?' Even as she spoke she was regretting the phrasing and wished she had asked what breed the mare was.

'She is not a valuable racehorse or anything like that, but to Steve, and I guess the rest of the family she is priceless. Etoile is her real name. She and Steve were a great team; he and Chloe spent more time in the saddle than out of it as teenagers. Gymkhanas, Pony Club, working stock on both properties, you name it, they did it. I would have thought she was getting a bit old to be having a first foal; guess that's why Steve is anxious about her.'

'Maybe he wants an excuse to keep her,' Eve suggested, remembering her own grief as a teenager when her father had sold her own beloved pony against all her entreaties. History had repeated itself when Harry, her husband, had sold Marion's outgrown pony, ignoring his daughter's tears. She felt a stab of guilt recalling that she had not opposed her husband, fearful as always of his criticism and over-anxious to appear 'sensible,' not the foolish, sentimental woman he often accused her of being. She could empathize with Steve.

'Yes, I think you are right.' Bill's voice

answering her recalled her to the present. 'He said she was too good *not* to breed from, that there would always be kids in the family needing a pony.'

'Yes.' Eve wished she had lived in a family that always had a place for an outgrown pony.

'Ah, good, I see someone has fed you.' Mary Malone, smiling warmly, brought Eve back to her present surroundings. 'How are you feeling, Bill? And Eve, are you over the flight, and how do you like Christmas in the sun?'

'It's wonderful!' Eve smiled back, captivated by her warmth even though she never waited for answers to her many questions.

'I've got champagne for the toast,' Mary said in a loud stage whisper. 'Maybe we will be able to wet the baby's head as well as toast the happy couple.'

'Happy couple?' Bill looked puzzled.

'Didn't Steve tell you? Well, isn't that just like a man for you!' Mary laughed and Bill looked anxious. 'Maureen and Gary are announcing their engagement.'

'Ahhh . . . that's great!' Bill smiled and looked genuinely happy for the young couple.

'Maureen is . . . ?' Eve began.

Mary cut in, 'My youngest daughter. Gary and Steve have been friends all their lives. We know him so well, he is already like another son. I thought once Gary and Chloe might pair off, then Chloe left home and — well — now it is Gary and Maureen.' She flashed them her warm and brilliant smile again. 'And now Chloe has brought a young man home.' She paused as if not quite sure about this development. 'He seems nice. I hope you like him, Bill?'

'Yes, well enough.' The tone of Bill's voice gave no clue to his feelings. As Mary turned away, Eve remembered the look on Chloe's face as she watched Maureen and Gary. Did she know that this Christmas day celebration was about to become an engagement party?

★ ★ ★

Chloe, with Adam a pace or so behind her, found Steve leaning on the gate to the little home paddock; she could see he was so tense he scarcely appeared to be breathing. As she joined him the mare lying in front of them gave a compulsive heave and a small replica of herself slithered on to the ground. A second later, the foal raised its head and its mother turned round to look at it. Then, incredibly, both were on their feet, Etty first then, after a few wobbly failures, the foal was searching for the milk bar. Its mother whickered softly as she turned to lick it.

'Ooh, she's perfect, and so like Etty!' Chloe breathed. Adam gave a shudder, wondering how much more life in the raw he would be exposed to over this holiday season. Unlike Chloe, he was repulsed rather than exalted by witnessing first-hand the miracle of birth. Neither she nor Steve noticed his reaction.

'Yes, she is a she, and exactly like her mother, even to the star on her head!' Steve's eyes shone with relief and exhilaration when he turned to Chloe. She smiled back, her delight matching his. Adam felt that he had become if not invisible then certainly surplus to the situation.

'What are you going to call her?' Chloe wanted to know.

'What do you think?' Steve hadn't thought that far. Chloe, he knew, loved finding apt names.

'She must have a Christmassy sort of name,' Chloe mused, 'or a star connection, after her mother, and because she has a star herself. I can only think of Christmas Star, but is that too obvious?'

'I think it is very suitable. That can be her official name, and at home she can be Chrissy.'

Chloe nodded her agreement and they remained leaning on the gate together, watching the foal, Adam temporarily forgotten.

'Wasn't that thrilling, just getting out here to see her born?' Chloe, remembering he had been with her when she came out, turned to include Adam in the excitement, her voice fading at the expression on his face.

'I can think of better thrills.'

Reminding herself that he was not a country person, Chloe bit back a sharp retort. 'Come on,' she said, taking his arm, 'let's go and celebrate with everyone else.'

Steve dragged his gaze from the foal to watch Chloe and Adam walking away. For a brief moment time had reversed and nothing had changed between Chloe and himself. With a last look at the mare and foal, he shrugged slightly as if shaking off a troublesome thought, and followed them back to the Christmas celebrations.

As Steve met his mother's eyes across the room he gave the thumbs-up sign. Mary Malone clapped her hands together then raised them in the air.

'We have a Christmas baby,' she announced. 'Etty has foaled and it's a — '

'Filly.' Steve interposed.

'And she is called . . . ' Mary paused again and once more Stephen filled in.

'Christmas Star.'

Eve joined in with the others as they clapped and applauded. Adam, she thought, was finding it hard to believe the birth of a horse could warrant champagne. She could see that the real cause for the popping corks was about to be announced when Mary raised her voice. 'We have a double celebration today.' She drew everyone's attention to her younger daughter holding hands with Gary Talbot. 'These two want you all to know they are going to tie the knot!'

There was a burst of applause and good wishes, some more than a little ribald. Eve smiled as she watched Maureen's pretty young face colour as she turned to look up at Gary, who drew her to him and, bending his head, kissed her long and lingeringly (to the sound of more cheers) on the lips. The champagne was poured and glasses passed round for a toast. It was then that Eve noticed Chloe, tight-lipped and unsmiling, staring into her glass, which she held so tightly Eve was afraid the stem might break. Then she squared her shoulders and with an overbright smile, raised her glass. Eve wondered if Adam had noticed anything — and if so how he felt.

Everybody wanted to go and see Christmas Star but Steve insisted that it was too much to expect the new mother to remain calm if the whole party trooped out at once so they dribbled out in twos and threes.

'Come on, Adam, come and look at the new baby.' Chloe reached out and took him by the hand.

'I've seen it, remember. We were there when it was born. Rather a fuss, isn't it, about a horse?'

'No, Etty is special, one of the family. She was Steve's special mount for all his growing-up years; he did Pony Club on her and everything else. Then when he got a bigger horse, his elder sister, Julie, had her for her kids. Now they are growing up, Steve decided to have her back and breed a foal from her.'

'I didn't ask for her life history,' Adam grumbled, then realizing he must sound very ungracious, he smiled, adding, 'I admit she looks like a nice horse, and the foal is kinda cute.'

Chloe sighed, wondering if inviting him had been such a good idea. Why hadn't someone told her that Gary and Maureen were an item? She called to Eve, 'Come and see the Christmas baby.'

Eve turned to Bill. 'Can you . . . ?' She glanced at his crutches.

'I daresay I could — with an effort. But I shall have plenty of opportunities to see her. You go along with Chloe.'

Eve didn't want to be reminded that her time here was temporary, but she forgot the slight feeling of rejection when she saw the beautiful foal who by now had mastered the intricacies of managing four long legs. 'Oh, but she is exquisite!' she cried in genuine admiration. 'All baby animals are gorgeous but newborn foals . . . ' Her voice petered out on a sigh as she searched her mind for the right superlative.

'I know,' Chloe agreed. 'There just isn't a word to do justice to them.'

Chloe found Eve, unlike Adam, genuinely interested in Etty's history. 'How good that you can keep her in the family.' Eve spoke with such feeling that Chloe looked at her sharply. Eve murmured, half to herself, 'It broke my heart when my father sold my pony.'

'You ride?' Chloe asked, surprised.

Eve shook her head. 'Not now. When I got into my teens, Dad sold my pony. He thought that ponies were toys you outgrew.' She tried to keep the bitterness at this remembered grief from her voice.

'A love of horses is something that stays with you all your life.' Chloe voiced aloud a conviction that had just become apparent. She thought with distaste of taking up a teaching post in the city when the long summer holidays finished.

They leaned on the railings, watching the new foal discovering this strange world she found herself in, the companionable silence broken by Chloe. 'Come and see Crispin,' she invited Eve. 'He's my horse,' she added. 'He lives here when I am away. He is a terrific stock horse and he gets used here, and he has company — other horses, I mean. If he stayed home he would be lonely and bored as well as getting fat.'

Eve followed Chloe towards the farm sheds, open-fronted ones full of farm machinery, and a tired and shabby wooden shed raised above the ground. The shearing shed, Eve deduced from the pungent smell of sheep. They all looked impermanent after the solid brick buildings she was used to on English farms.

Chloe led the way to a yard with a water trough at one end and a large tree at the other. Its hanging branches were symmetrically levelled at the bottom, giving the impression of a huge shade umbrella. As they drew closer, Eve caught a whiff of a tangy scent not a bit like the one she was beginning to associate with trees. Eve pointed at it. 'Why do you trim it like that?' she asked Chloe.

'We don't, the horses and cattle do; they nibble the bottom of the branches when they are standing underneath it.'

'I'm not surprised, if it tastes as good as it smells. What sort of tree is it?'

'A peppercorn tree.' Chloe pointed at the small pinkish red balls hanging in bunches. 'They are not a native tree, they originally came from America, I believe. In some areas they are considered a weed and one is not supposed to plant them but I don't think anyone bothers about big established trees like this fellow.'

'A weed!'

'A weed is just a plant in the wrong place,' Chloe pointed out with a smile, shading her eyes to peer out towards a clump of gum trees. With her two front fingers in her mouth, she whistled. At the piercing sound three horses emerged from the shade of the trees and when Chloe whistled again they trotted towards them.

'I am impressed.' Eve was awestruck.

Chloe smiled her pleasure at the compliment. 'Steve taught me to do that,' she admitted. 'His grandfather taught him; he was a horse breaker.'

The three horses were now at the fence; Chloe was reaching out to rub their foreheads and let them snuffle softly at her free hand. 'This is Crispin.' She drew Eve's attention to a small grey, his rocking-horse dapples fading to white with middle age. 'Dad bought him for my twelfth birthday. You name it and he and I have done it together.' Her voice rang with affection and pride. 'The palomino here is Steve's horse. He is called Golden Dollar because of his colour. It gets abbreviated to Dolly, which tends to confuse everyone about his sex.' Chloe laid her hand on the neck of an old black mare with a spattering of grey hairs round her eyes. 'This old girl is Midnight. She belongs to Julie, Steve's eldest sister. Her pet name is Minnie. Julie won a lot of ribbons with her before she was married.'

Eve loved horses but Chloe, she could see, had a passion for them. 'How can you bear leaving them to work in the city?' The words were out before she stopped to think.

'I am not sure that I can.' Chloe spoke softly, almost to herself.

For a moment Chloe looked so bereft that Eve wished she had not spoken, but when Chloe turned her smile was as bright as ever. 'Well, there you are — that's our horses. If you want to ride I am sure Julie wouldn't mind lending you old Minnie.' She turned away to give Crispin a last stroke before leading the way back to the Christmas celebrations.

The party appeared to be winding down. Children were getting fretful and Mary was making tea and coffee. Bill, Eve thought, looked tired. 'Chloe took me to see the horses,' she told him as she sat down.

'Yes, I saw you heading that way. Do you like horses?'

'Yes, I love them. I had a pony as a child but my father sold him when I outgrew him.' She sighed. 'I'm afraid the same thing happened to my daughter.' She thought Chloe was lucky to still have Crispin.

'I would never sell Crispin even though Chloe is home so little to ride him. I know she loves him.'

'Yes — I think she misses him.'

Bill wondered what Chloe had said to Eve but said nothing but 'Thanks!' to Steve, who appeared in front of them with a mug of coffee in each hand.

'When you are ready . . . ' Steve said tentatively as he handed the older man coffee. 'No hurry, mind.' He wanted to make it clear that he was available when he needed him for a lift home but certainly didn't want to sound as if he was hassling him.

Bill drained his cup and put it down. 'I am ready now,' he said, adding to Eve with wry humour, 'I guess sitting around must be more tiring than running around. But you don't have to leave, you can come back with Chloe.'

Eve shook her head. 'I'd rather come with

you.' It had been an enjoyable day but she too was tired.

In the car, Eve let the desultory chat between the two men flow over and around her as she watched the brown paddocks fenced by wire and punctuated here and there by gaunt eucalyptus slide past the windows If she lived here a hundred years, she reflected, she would never get used to Christmas in mid-summer.

4

'Oh!' Eve gasped as a flock of grey birds rose from the ground revealing brilliant rosy pink underbellies. 'Are those parrots?'

'Galahs — pink galahs. They are common round here,' Steve told her.

'I was amazed to see them change colour as they flew up.' Eve thought flocks of parrots might take as much getting used to as Christmas in summer.

'They are quite drab compared with some of our parrots,' Bill said from the back seat. 'Rosellas are really colourful — bright green, red and yellow — but usually seen in pairs. You sometimes see sulphur-crested cockatoos in big flocks. They are popular as pets because they are good talkers, but I am afraid they are more often seen as pests than pets.'

'Why is that?'

'For the damage they do to crops,' Bill explained. 'But those galahs were probably eating the seeds of noxious weeds,' he added, seeing her crestfallen expression.

'I remember seeing a sulphur-crested cockatoo in a pet shop when I was a child,' Eve remembered. 'He was chained to a perch and muttering to himself. People were getting closer and closer to him trying to hear what he said, and when he had a good crowd really close he let out a raucous shriek that made them all jump back, then he rocked on his perch and chortled.'

'Smart devils, cockys,' Steve remarked.

'I felt sorry for him, chained on that little perch all day,' Eve admitted. 'Even more now I know something of his natural environment.'

'You have a soft heart.' Bill grunted. 'Fancy a cuppa?' he asked Steve as he propped his crutches against his favourite armchair.

'No, thanks all the same. Stock still need tending even on Christmas Day.'

'And there is that new foal to check on. You be off. Thanks for the lift.'

'Yes, thanks,' said Eve. 'And for a lovely day. I have really enjoyed it; please tell your mother.'

'I'll be off, then.' He moved to the door, hesitated, then turned to Eve. 'Chloe said you might like to ride one day?'

'Well, thank you, yes, but I haven't ridden for years.'

'Old Midnight is just about bomb-proof.'

Eve was relieved to hear that; she viewed the prospect with mixed feelings but smiled. 'Thanks — I'll look forward to it.'

He nodded. 'Right, I'll be off,' he repeated, and this time went.

Eve looked vaguely round, wondering how to fill the silence.

'Would you like a cup of tea?' she finally asked. 'I'm sure I can find the things and make you one.'

'Good idea!' Both forgot they had had a drink just before they left the Malones'. Eve filled up the electric jug and Bill told her where to find teabags and mugs.

'Christmas food is great but a good cup of tea takes some beating.' He smiled as she handed him his tea a few minutes later.

'Absolutely. I shall always remember this Christmas, everyone was so friendly.' She grinned. 'And the food was unforgettable!'

After a pause in which Bill, Eve thought, was either lost in his own thoughts or debating what to say next, he startled her by asking, 'Have you met Adam before?'

'B-before?' was all she could manage to stammer in confusion.

'Yes, before you met him here.' Bill enunciated the words slowly and clearly and kept his eyes on her face.

Eve shook her head vigorously. 'No — no, of course not!' She felt herself flush with indignation and hoped he wouldn't think she was lying, but what was he suggesting?

'I get the feeling there is something funny, and I do not mean just the coincidence of your names, something I do not know about.' He was still watching her closely. Eve knew that some sort of explanation was necessary before he sent his imagination into full flight.

'It was — there was — on the night I arrived, there was a sort of — well — a bit of a misunderstanding.'

'He arrived the same evening as you? Did you meet on the journey or something?'

Eve shook her head, wishing that it were so simple.

'Not exactly. We met when he arrived here. It was all a stupid mistake — a misunderstanding, best forgotten.'

'I can't forget what I don't know,' Bill pointed out, reasonably enough. 'I think you should explain.'

'It was just a silly misunderstanding,' Eve mumbled, hoping that Bill would let it go, but one glance at his set features convinced her there was little hope of that.

'Why didn't you tell Chloe about me?' Attack was, she decided, the best form of defence. Nonplussed, Bill shrugged. 'She didn't tell me she had invited Adam.'

'He turned up very late. Chloe thought he wasn't coming at all that night so she sent me to the spare bedroom. When he turned up in the middle of the night he misunderstood her directions or something and ended up in my room.' Eve shrugged, as if to signify 'end of story', but Bill waited for her to continue.

'You woke up and redirected him?' he prompted.

'Well, not exactly. Actually, I screamed. Chloe appeared in the doorway and was, well, a bit annoyed.'

'But surely she was as much to blame as anyone?' Bill looked at her quizzically, waiting for an explanation.

'We, we — neither of us had — It was so hot,' Eve finally stammered. Eyes downcast, she did not see the grin slowly spreading across Bill's face.

'Poor Adam hadn't even got his fig leaf, and you . . . ?'

Eve nodded. 'Chloe rather lost her cool; she was wild with Adam and accused me — ' Embarrassed to admit what Chloe had actually said, she stopped, but Bill was determined to hear everything.

'She accused you . . . ?' he prompted.

'Oh, just of wanting all you men — Steve, you and Adam.'

'To think I was stuck in hospital and missed all the fun! Chloe seems OK with you now. I thought you seemed to be getting on well together.'

'Oh, yes, but we did get off to rather a bad start. When Steve brought me out here she seemed to think I had picked him up somewhere. She seemed to think I had engineered being met at the station by Steve and — well — she was very dubious that I knew you. She said I couldn't have met you on the Internet because you hadn't got a computer and if you had one you wouldn't be able to work it. Why on earth didn't you tell her, Bill?'

'She thought I was too dumb to use a computer . . . I wanted to surprise her with my new-found skill.'

'I'm not talking about the computer. Why didn't you tell her I was coming for Christmas?'

'Same reason, I suppose, that she didn't tell me about Adam.' Bill growled. 'Then I fell off that damn truck before I had a chance to explain. What did you think of the Malones?' Bill asked with a sudden change of subject.

'I liked them all — very much indeed. You are lucky to have such good neighbours, but . . . ' Eve trailed off, feeling she should keep her opinions to herself on such a short acquaintance.

'But . . . ?' Bill echoed.

'Why on earth did Chloe invite Adam here

71

when Steve Malone is so obviously nuts about her?'

Bill sighed. 'You can see that, I can see it, probably everyone but Chloe can. She acts as if he was her best pal — nothing more.'

'Unfortunately we can't run our adult children's lives for them,' Eve pointed out.

'More's the pity — we might make a better job of it than they do themselves.' He sighed gustily. 'Any more tea in that pot?'

Eve lifted the lid. 'Not much — I'll boil up the jug again.' She smiled at Bill as she sat down a few minutes later and refilled both their mugs.

'I'm glad you came, Eve.' He was cradling the mug of hot tea and looking down at it; he spoke in a soft voice and Eve, in a reverie of her own, did not realize for a moment that he had spoken to her.

'Yes, me too. I've always wanted to see Australia but it seemed so far away — in every way.'

'I had hoped to take you around, show you places, but . . . ' His voice trailed off but his angry gesture towards his plastered ankle said it all.

'You could suggest places for me to go to,' Eve pointed out. 'I thought I might hire a car.'

'No need to do that, you can borrow mine.

Is there anything you are particularly interested in?'

'Not just touristy, I want to see something of the real Australia — not the shop front decorated for outsiders. I've enjoyed the time I have spent here so much. But I couldn't do that, borrow your car, I mean — you might need it.'

'You have only been here a couple of days,' he protested, 'and at holiday time when we are all on our best behaviour. There is lots to see and do round here; I wouldn't have offered the use of my car if I hadn't thought you a sensible and responsible person.'

Eve wasn't too sure she was flattered by his assessment but it was a generous offer. She nodded. 'Thank you, Bill, that is kind of you. I do have a current driver's licence and a clean record.' She was thoughtful for a moment. 'Maybe I'll take up Steve's offer of a chance to ride.'

Bill broke the silence with a noisy yawn. 'Sorry — it isn't the company. Champagne on top of good food, I guess. Christmas with a broken leg seems to have knocked me out.' He smiled ruefully at Eve, his lids heavy.

'You stood up to it well,' Eve assured him, fighting to suppress a yawn herself. 'Why don't you have forty winks?' She got up to take their cups over to the sink. 'I think I will follow your example; I'm not quite sure I am fully orientated after the flight.'

In her room she kicked off her shoes, picked up the glossy magazine she had bought at the airport and barely glanced at, puffed up the pillows behind her and stretched her legs out on the bed. As she idly flicked the pages, she remembered that she had bought it because it featured an article on interior design, but before she found the piece she was looking for her eyes dropped shut and the magazine slid out of her fingers to lie on the bed at her side.

She woke up to the sound of people — voices, laughter, footsteps — and a feeling of utter confusion. Where on earth was she? Her eyes swivelled to the door and she saw that what had actually woken her was the sound of it opening.

'Hope I didn't disturb you,' Chloe remarked cheerfully, quite obviously, Eve thought even in her fuddled state, telling a lie. 'But we are back and even Dad is awake. He said you were probably still zonked out.

Eve swung her legs over the side of the bed and sat up, blinking to clear this unflattering picture of herself. 'I've had a lovely rest and I'm wide awake now, thanks.' She bent down to pick up the magazine that had fallen to the floor and swung it round on to the bed rather too vigorously. It slid along to drop on the floor in front of Chloe. It fell open at the piece she had meant to read before falling asleep.

'Have you read this?' Chloe asked, stabbing the open page with a forefinger.

'Not yet. I dropped off to sleep.'

'It is by Fern Barclay. She is quite well known as an interior designer. She lives not far away and did up a house for someone I know,' Chloe told her as she tossed the magazine back on the bed. 'I came to see if you were awake as we are about to have a 'plates and forks on our knees' snack supper. See you out there in a few minutes. Sorry I disturbed you but I thought you might be getting hungry.'

Eve was surprised to find herself ready to consider food again, and after a quick freshen up headed for the sound of voices and laughter.

When Bill smiled and patted the sofa at his side, it gave her a fuzzy glow inside. 'Have a good snooze?' he enquired with a wide smile.

'Great — how about you?' She thought this was the first time she had seen him smile like that, with his whole face. 'You look whole heaps better,' she told him.

'That's probably because I feel it. Oh, this plaster is still as unwieldy and heavy but my leg isn't really painful any more, just a nuisance, and I feel I am getting to grips with these damn things.' He indicated the crutches propped up against the end of the sofa. 'If not exactly mastering them,' he added.

'I think you have come to grips wonderfully with the whole situation.' Eve spoke with sincerity. 'If it had been me I would have freaked out altogether.'

'I doubt it. You strike me as a coper rather than a freaker-outer.'

'You have more faith in me than I have in myself.' She smiled ruefully.

'Perhaps you underestimate yourself. You know what they say: If you think you can't, or you think you can, you are right.'

'Well, I thought I could come out to Australia on my own, and here I am!'

'Yes, here you are, and I think another challenge is on its way.'

Eve looked up and saw Steve heading towards her. 'Chloe says how about riding in the morning?'

'I haven't ridden for years — not since I was a child,' Eve stammered, on the verge of refusing. She glanced at Bill, remembering their recent conversation.

'You'll find you haven't forgotten,' he assured her. 'You will be stiff next day though!'

'I guess you are right — on both counts.' Eve turned from Bill to Steve. 'What time?'

'Come over when you and Chloe feel like it. Make it before the day warms up.' He grinned at Bill. 'You can entertain Adam. I'm sure he would rather have your company than horses.'

'Or cows,' Bill retorted with a deadpan expression.

'You told Steve about Adam's little accident out with the cow?'

'But of course.' Bill looked innocent. 'Steve needed cheering up.'

Eve smiled. From her own observation she was sure that learning that Adam had put himself in such a bad light with Chloe would be pleasing.

Several of the younger Malones had come back to the McMahons', including Maureen and Gary Talbot. Chloe had laid out a buffet supper on the kitchen bench along with a cask of wine and a pack of stubbies. A CD was playing in the background and Eve found herself listening with one ear to what Bill was saying and to the music with the other; a woman singing a country ballad in a slightly husky voice. She thought this was the third time she had seen Chloe replenish her glass from the wine cask.

'I know I shouldn't be saying I feel hungry

after the feast the Malones put on but I wouldn't say no to a nice cold beer and a snack.' Bill claimed her attention.

'Neither would I,' Eve admitted. 'Stay there and I'll go and get us both something.'

'I'm not planning to go anywhere.' Bill jerked his head at his plaster.

'Do you like country music?' Adam asked her as she joined him at the counter.

'Yes, yes, I do. I like this singer too. Who is it?'

'Fiona Cameron,' Chloe cut in. 'You may have heard her. She is a local person — doesn't live far from here.'

'Chloe is a devoted fan, her unofficial publicity agent.' The tone of Adam's voice caused Chloe to flash him a look of annoyance. 'She *is* good, but I count myself a friend more than a fan.' She turned to Eve. 'I have known her for quite a while. She is a very nice person as well as being a good singer.'

'I like that slight huskiness in her voice and I also like being able to hear every word. I'd like to get one of her CDs to take home.'

Chloe looked delighted. 'I'll lend you mine to listen to here,' she promised, adding, 'Put plenty of chutney on Dad's plate. Do you both want a drink?'

'He asked for a beer but I think I would

78

like some of that wine you seem to be enjoying.'

Chloe shrugged. 'If you take the food I'll bring the drinks over.' She followed Eve across the room and put the drinks down on the side table with the food.

'Have you enjoyed Christmas, Dad?' she asked. 'In spite of everything.'

'Probably *because* of everything. I have never been waited on so well in all my life.'

'I have forgiven you now for not telling me about Eve, especially as she has turned out to be such a nice person, not a whingeing Pom,' Eve suspected that the red wine was loosening Chloe's tongue.

'In that case, I suppose I must also forgive you for not telling me about Adam,' Bill retorted.

'What is a whingeing Pom?, other than something that I must be grateful for not being?' Eve asked him as Chloe moved back to the younger people.

'Well, a Pom, or Pommie, is an English person and I am sorry to say some have a bit of a reputation for grumbling about things here — whingeing.'

'But what do they find to whinge about? So far I have thought everything great out here. Different, but good.'

'Plenty — the weather for one thing.'

'But the English always talk about the weather.'

'The main complaint from those who do whinge is that things are not the same as in England.'

'But that is absurd; how could anyone expect to cross the world and expect everything the same as they left behind?'

Bill smiled. 'True. I haven't heard you whinge once — or mention the weather.'

'That is because I am really enjoying this extra summer. If I were at home it would be winter. You seem so much better. I was afraid that . . . well . . . you seem to have enjoyed today.' Her voice trailed away as she almost voiced thoughts best kept to herself. Eve flushed, suddenly aware that Bill expected her to continue her train of thought. 'Well, I wasn't really sure . . . I mean, when you said . . . '

'Oh, Eve! I owe you an apology. You were right in thinking that I wished you hadn't come, but that was nothing to do with you and all to do with me. I didn't want you to meet me like this, a crippled old man, I wanted to be able to take you out to places, do things with you, show you around. Especially when I saw you. You look younger than I expected; now I know you better . . . ' He left the sentence in mid-air.

'I'm forty; I have never told you any different. And you are forty-five, not an old man at all. Anyone, at any age, can break their ankle. Our friendship is of the mind . . . ' Hearing herself, she stopped again in mid-sentence. She sounded positively pompous. When she saw the twinkle in Bill's eyes, in spite of his serious expression, she relaxed. 'Sorry, I sound school-marmy,' she admitted.

'Somewhat,' he agreed, but his smile removed any censure. 'I must admit if I could have stopped you coming I probably would have done; but as I didn't let's drink to my failure!'

'Do you mind if I ride tomorrow?'

'No — no, of course not. Go ahead — there is no better way of seeing the country. I only wish I could come with you. But while you are gone I will put my thinking cap on and work out something we can do together.'

Eve almost wished he had said he would mind, she had little confidence in her own equestrian ability.

★ ★ ★

When Eve, dressed in jeans and sneakers, made her way to the kitchen at breakfast time, Chloe and Adam were arguing, and there was no sign of any breakfast.

'Good morning.' She spoke hesitantly.

'*She* knows about cows — get her to help you. But don't ask me to ever go near the filthy beast again.' Adam ignored her greeting but not her presence.

'Do you need my help?' Eve spoke directly to Chloe.

'Yes,' Chloe rapped, adding a belated, 'Please.'

Helping, Eve learned, meant getting the cow into the stall and washing her udder while Chloe measured out the food and watching while Chloe milked. 'I used to find milking rather therapeutic. Do you?' Eve remarked as the milk jets pinged into the bucket from the cow's full udder.

'I suppose I do.' Chloe, her head buried in the cow's flank so that her voice was slightly muffled, agreed. 'Sorry for dragging you out here, without your breakfast, but Adam is useless.'

'Why did you invite him here, Chloe?' Eve finally asked into the lengthening silence now punctuated not by jets of milk pinging against the side of a bucket but the soft splash as they landed in a bucket containing several litres of milk.

'In a moment of madness,' Chloe muttered

into the cow's flank. 'I was sorry for him when I realized he had nowhere to go over Christmas and I thought he might be useful.'

'Useful?'

Chloe looked shamefaced. 'It was stupid. I thought bringing a boyfriend home . . . '

Eve knew what she meant, her reaction when she realized Gary and Maureen were engaged had said it all.

'I must have been drunk when I asked him.'

'Take more water with it next time,' Eve advised, 'or you might get yourself into something you really can't get out of!'

'I will!' Chloe promised, raising the lever to allow the cow to walk out of the stall. 'Guard that milk with your life' — she pointed to the fresh milk, — 'while I let the calf in with her.' When she added, 'I think he has to be back in the New Year,' it was a few minutes before Eve realized that it was Adam she meant.

She wondered if they would manage to get through the time without a major row as Adam watched Chloe pouring the milk into a large bowl. 'What are you doing with that?' he asked suspiciously.

'Setting it so that I can skim the cream off,' Chloe told him.

'What does that mean?'

'Tomorrow I will skim the cream off and

we can use the milk.'

Adam looked astonished. 'You mean you — drink — that?'

'Of course we do. What do you think we do, pour it down the sink?'

'But isn't it — I mean, is it *safe*?'

'Well, it hasn't killed Dad off yet, and he has drunk it most of his life,' Chloe snapped as she placed the pan carefully in the huge fridge.

'What has Dad been drinking all his life?' Bill manoeuvred himself and his crutches awkwardly and noisily to a chair at the kitchen table.

He looked relieved when Chloe said milk. He smiled at Eve.

'I thought you were telling Eve I was a heavy whisky drinker.'

'Adam would think that preferable,' Chloe told him, leaving Bill to look to Eve for some sort of explanation. She merely shrugged, but when she smiled at him he noted the gleam of amusement in her eyes whereas that Adam fellow looked as if he had just sucked a lemon. Not for the first time, he wondered why Chloe had invited him, as she seemed to be making little effort to be pleasant to him. Somehow he thought it very unlikely he would be asked to accept him as a son-in-law.

5

Chloe looked Eve over critically. To the jeans, sneakers and shirt that were the most suitable riding clothes in her luggage, she had added a straw hat, which she was dangling from its cord. 'Are those the only shoes you have?'

'Well, no, they are just the ones I thought most suitable.'

'Hmm, well, they are not very safe. You need boots with heels. Those could slip through the stirrup and you might get dragged.'

Eve quailed; to be dragged she had to be thrown first. She stared at Chloe. 'Seven — or seven and a half,' she muttered in response to the query, 'What size shoes do you take?'

'Same size as me.' Chloe disappeared and came back carrying a pair of brown leather elastic-sided boots. 'They are a bit old and could do with a clean but they should fit you. I have another pair.'

'They seem fine, thank you,' Eve murmured as she sat down on the nearest chair and pulled on the boots. She stood up, feeling at least two inches taller in the heels, and picked up her hat. But Chloe had not finished.

'You can't wear that hat,' she told her firmly. 'You need a safety helmet.' She produced what looked like a motorcyclist's helmet. 'See if this fits you. I had it in Pony Club.' Without ceremony she rammed it down on Eve's head, fiddled with the chinstrap to adjust it correctly and snapped it closed. 'There!' she said with some satisfaction. 'You should be OK now.'

'Thank you,' Eve said. What sort of a monster were they intending to put her on that she needed so much safety equipment? In actual fact she felt anything but OK. The heels of her boots felt very high and her head felt heavier than the rest of her. Added to which the emphasis on safety had done nothing to booster her flagging confidence. 'What about you?' she asked Chloe. 'What are you going to wear if I have your safety helmet?'

'Oh, I'll wear my good old Akubra,' she said jauntily. 'I hate wearing helmets.' She went to the line of pegs on the veranda and pulled off what looked like a somewhat shabby Wild West hat. It had a huge brim and a drawstring under the chin, and looked shady, serviceable and comfortable. Eve wished she were wearing it.

'That looks better!' Chloe told Eve, running her eyes quickly over her. 'Come on — we had better get moving. Steve will be waiting for us. Probably all saddled up.'

He was in the stock-yard when they got there but the saddles were on the railings not the horses' backs. 'Hi!' he greeted them cheerfully. 'That's Midnight's gear.' He nodded in the direction of what looked to Eve to be a very large and complicated pile of saddlery astride the rough railings of the yard, picked up another similar pile and clapped it down on his own horse. As Chloe was doing the same to Crispin, Eve moved tentatively forward and with an effort hauled the heavy saddle off the fence, and murmured soothing nothings to the elderly black mare securely tied to one of the fence posts.

The saddle was quite unlike the relatively flat English saddle she had been used to as a child. It had a deep rounded seat with a high pommel and cantle. A mohair webbing girth went round the horse's belly and a surcingle girth round the saddle itself. The stirrups were heavy aluminum in a shape she had never seen before. She later learned they were called Oxbows.

With his own horse saddled and Chloe about to mount Crispin, Steve helped Eve bridle the old mare and after checking she had the girths fastened tightly enough, held Midnight still while Eve clambered, awkwardly and inelegantly, into the unfamiliar saddle. 'I think the stirrup leathers need shortening,' she suggested tentatively.

'Give them a go first,' Steve advised. 'That is an Australian stock saddle you have there; you need to sit right down in it so your stirrups should be a bit longer than you are used to with an English saddle. Tell me how you feel when we have been going for a bit.'

Eve found he was right, and the saddle was about the most comfortable thing she had ever sat in on a horse — more than comfortable, she felt secure in it, so much so that she was sure the helmet that was making her feel top-heavy was unnecessary. Midnight was a well-schooled horse with perfect manners; Eve relaxed and prepared to enjoy herself.

'Why do you call all the fields paddocks?' she asked as they rode across a large expanse of brown grass on which equally brown sheep grazed, blurring into the background.

'Because that's what they are.' Chloe looked puzzled at the question.

'But they are so big,' Eve protested. 'A paddock in England is a small place near the farm buildings, used for — well, things that need to be near home. The horse, the house cow, those sorts of animals. The rest are called fields.'

'Small areas round the homestead usually get called yards here.'

'Words and names always interest me,' Eve reflected. 'Well, language and languages. If we who speak the same language can get confused no wonder there are problems when different languages are involved.' Eve gave herself a mental shake; she had done enough philosophizing which could well be taken for preaching.

Steve led the way up a slight rise which gave them a good view of the surrounding countryside. 'I suppose all these wire fences look awful to you?'

'Not really,' Eve answered.

'But whenever I look at pictures of English farms the paddocks — sorry, fields — are divided by thick hedges.'

'Not any more.' Eve shook her head. 'Hawthorn hedge fences are getting fewer; we are seeing larger fields and more barbed wire. I suppose it is a worldwide trend.' Her sigh became a smile. 'I love your gum trees; they are such a soft green against the brilliant blue sky.'

Steve pointed out the homestead. 'That's our place.' He turned in the saddle and pointed in the opposite direction.

'And that's ours,' Chloe told her. 'If there was a gate in the fence it would be nearer to visit this way, by horse, than by road.'

Eve noticed that instead of the farmhouses clustering together to form small hamlets, each one seemed to be placed in the centre of its own land.

'Is there a village or do you have to go to Bendigo for everything?'

'There is, only we don't use that word much either,' Chloe told her. 'There is the little township of Goornong only a mile or so away. It boasts a store and post office, a school and the ubiquitous pub, and that is about it. With the drift away from the country many of these small places have shrunk rather than grown over the years. I guess the car is partly responsible for that — it only takes about thirty minutes at most to get to Bendigo.' She stopped abruptly, feeling, as Eve had done, that she was in danger of delivering a lecture.

Steve glanced down at his watch, turned his horse homeward and they rode back for the most part in a companionable silence.

'Enjoy yourself?' Bill asked as Eve flopped down into one of the kitchen chairs, pulling off the borrowed riding helmet as she did so. She pushed back her damp hair. 'It's getting hot, and my legs feel as if they will be permanently bowed,' she told him, 'but, yes, I did enjoy myself very much. I felt I was really experiencing Australia.'

Bill smiled but all he said was, 'It's better in the autumn when it rains; at this time of the year it is dry and dusty.'

'Yes.' Eve could only agree as she struggled to pull off the dusty riding boots she had worn. 'Sorry?' she added as she realized Bill was asking her a question.

'How were the other two?' he repeated.

'Steve and Chloe?' It seemed to her an odd question.

Before she could reply, Chloe appeared and threw herself down in an armchair. 'It's getting hot,' she remarked, stating what was becoming increasingly obvious. 'Hope you enjoyed it, Eve. I can't say Steve was exactly a ball of laughs, can you?'

'He seemed OK to me, but then I don't know him well.' Eve was diplomatic.

'If he couldn't be bothered to be pleasant he should have left us to ride on our own.'

Eve had been too busy getting to know her mount while admiring the unfamiliar scenery to take much notice of the other two, but now she thought about it maybe there had been a stressed atmosphere between them; conversation directed at her rather than each other. She stood up. 'I had better change.'

'Have a shower if you like,' Chloe told her, 'but keep it short.'

'I will.' Eve had already learned that as all their water came from the large rainwater tanks alongside the house, it was not something you used extravagantly.

'I'll have one after you,' Chloe called after her as she left the room.

*　*　*

'Just coming . . . ' Eve saw the handle of the bathroom door move as she stepped out of the shower. She wrapped the huge bath towel round herself before cautiously opening the door, clothes in hand, to dress in her own room and not keep Chloe waiting, but it was Adam on the other side of the door. 'What's the hurry?' she asked.

Adam's eyes slid over her but Eve was not sure whether it was with appreciation or something else. She felt a tremor ripple up her spine and tried to pull the bath towel back into place.

She dressed quickly and was surprised when she glanced through the window to see Adam leaning on the gate outside, apparently lost in thought. She decided he looked troubled and was half-tempted to go and ask why. Crushing the impulse, she left her room to join Bill. He was standing, leaning on his crutches, looking frustrated, but he smiled when he saw her.

'You seem to be mastering those things pretty well now.'

'It's a slow business,' he grumbled. 'I was heading for a cold beer. I'm sure you could use one too.' Leaving her to get them, he added, 'Bring them out on to the veranda, it's cooler there.'

'Just what I needed.' Eve sighed as she took the first sip of her beer. When Chloe appeared a few moments later, she immediately turned back into the house to collect one for herself. Across the yard, still with his back to them, Adam unlatched the gate.

'Hope he shuts it properly,' Chloe muttered. They watched him turn back to the latch, then, without glancing in their direction, stride off across the paddock. 'And any other gate he goes through,' Chloe added.

'Oh, I am sure he will,' Eve said soothingly, wondering where Adam was heading. 'Even if he isn't cow-wise he must surely realize that you always leave gates as you find them.'

'I hope you are right but cow-wise isn't all he isn't — he isn't country-wise at all.' Chloe looked sour as she watched Adam's retreating figure.

'Well surely you knew something about

him before you asked him here?'

'Not really, Dad.' Eve also wondered about what seemed a rather odd relationship but unlike him did not feel she was in a position to ask direct questions. As they watched him, Adam reached the gate on the far side of the paddock, hesitated for a few moments then turned round and began to stroll back.

'I thought he probably wouldn't go any further. The steers are in that paddock.' Chloe sighed with satisfaction.

'When you asked him here for Christmas I thought you must have known him for a while — that maybe it was serious.'

'Well, you thought wrong, Dad. Anyway, who are you to talk?'

They seemed to have forgotten she was sitting with them, Eve thought, waiting for Chloe to ask her father if he was serious about her. She gulped down the last of her beer. 'I — I'll check he fastens the gate properly,' she told them as she jumped to her feet.

Adam looked surprised but not displeased as she joined him.

'I needed to stretch my legs,' she explained, noting that he had latched the gate.

'Same here, I feel a bit like a bug under a microscope. But I should have thought you had taken enough exercise today.'

'I know how you feel.' Indeed she did; she felt that everyone she met was speculating on her relationship with Bill.

Adam threw her a quick sympathetic glance but lost in her own thoughts, she was unaware of it. 'You don't put your foot in it as often as I do.' His voice was gloomy.

'I was brought up on a farm, even if it was in England, so I'm a bit more country-conscious. What made you come? I mean . . . ' She floundered. 'It isn't as if you and . . . ' Her voice faded out.

'It isn't as if Chloe and I are an item.' He said it for her. 'When she asked me it seemed a good idea; we had just enjoyed a pleasant evening together and I had nowhere else to go for Christmas, and . . . ' He grinned sheepishly. 'I had probably had too much to drink.'

Eve remembered Chloe had said the same thing about herself. 'Perhaps you both had.' Her tone was dry.

She wondered what he intended to do now but before she could phrase the question he said, 'I guess I shall just move on now and fade gracefully out of Chloe's life. What about you? Are things working out for you as you hoped?'

'What do you mean?' Eve's voice was sharp, she had no intention of disclosing her inner feelings to Adam.

'You must have been hoping for something to take off to come to the other side of the world on the strength of an Internet friendship.'

Eve bridled at his tone and the suggestion in his words. 'I was not expecting anything more than a short holiday in a country I have always wanted to visit.' Eve did her best to sound frosty. She wanted to add, '*And what about you? What were you hoping for?*' She bit her tongue and began to walk back to the house but he caught her by the arm and rather than be seen having an undignified scuffle with him, she stood still, muttering in a tight voice, 'Please let go of me.'

'Only if you listen to me and don't rush off.'

She shook her arm free. 'Make it brief.'

'You are very attractive and you also seem very nice. I know I'm out of line giving you advice, but — well, don't do anything rash.'

'Such as?' she all but snapped.

'Burning your boats.'

'I think I could get to like it here.' She glared at him. 'This is somewhat premature — and mere speculation at that. If you have quite finished?' Turning sharply away, she hurried towards the house. In spite of his interference, she remembered that he had said she was attractive.

She climbed the steps of the veranda, feeling that she was under scrutiny, but Bill was lost in his own thoughts and Chloe had Eve's magazine in her hand. It was still folded back to the page on interior design.

'Were you reading this?'

Eve nodded. 'It is a subject that has always interested me; I almost did a course in it once.'

'What stopped you?' Bill asked.

'Oh, life in general, I suppose,' Eve answered vaguely, remembering the many objections that Harry had made, so many in fact that it just hadn't seemed worth the bother of going against him. As she had so often done in her marriage, she simply gave in and dropped the idea. She turned back to Chloe who, she realized, was saying something to her about the piece in the magazine.

'The woman who wrote this — Fern Barclay — did up Fiona's house for her.'

'Do you mean Fiona Cameron, the singer?' She remembered Chloe had said she knew her.

'Yes, that's right. She bought an old farmhouse not far from here. It was a mess but she had heard Fern was a wizard at that sort of thing and when she found she had actually bought a cottage in the area and done it up for herself she went to see her and persuaded her to take on her house. She transformed it. If you are interested I could take you over to meet Fiona and see Fern's ideas put into practice.'

'That sounds marvellous — two celebrities in one hit!'

'Well, sort of. You will only be seeing Fern's work, not her, and I can't guarantee we will see Fiona — she is often away on tour — but she lives with her brother so if he is home we will be able to see the house.' She turned to her father. 'You come too, Dad — an outing would do you good.' She looked up as Adam rejoined them. 'And you too, Adam. Let's all go. I'll give Fiona a call and find out when it will be convenient.' Without waiting for an answer, she jumped up and ran inside to the phone.

Eve turned to Bill eagerly. 'You will come along, won't you?' She touched his arm lightly with the tips of her fingers, needing to prove something to Adam.

'But of course. I can hop about now. We could make a day of it — show you a bit of the countryside, have lunch out . . . ' he turned to Adam. 'You, too, of course.'

'Thank you, I would like to see the country round about while I am here.'

'We are in luck!' Chloe was beaming as she

rejoined them. 'Fiona is home at the moment — said she would love to see us. Nothing she likes better than showing off her house. She suggests coffee tomorrow; she has to go to Melbourne later on in the day.'

'Could I listen to some of Fiona's CDs this afternoon?' Eve wanted to be reasonably knowledgeable before she met the singer. 'I will reread that piece about Fern too.'

They set off the following morning as soon as breakfast and the chores were finished, Chloe driving with her father in the front passenger seat as he found it easier for his plastered ankle. This left Eve to share the back seat with Adam. Compensating for the frisson of annoyance that still lingered after their conversation the previous day, she smiled brightly as she climbed in by him.

They turned on to the Northern Highway at the little township of Goornong and Eve looked about her with interest, remembering that Chloe had told her that this was actually their nearest place. There was, as she had said, a shop, a post office and a pub all fronting the highway.

'I see what you mean about Goornong,' she remarked to Chloe, 'but where are the houses?'

'Mostly behind the highway,' Bill told her. 'There is a little more than meets the eye as you drive through — school, swimming pool, church and police station.'

For the next ten minutes or so they drove up a long straight highway and into another small town that to Eve looked like a larger Goornong, as it seemed to be laid out in much the same manner. When Chloe turned off the main road and then turned again into one of the parallel streets, Bill asked her, 'Where are you going? I didn't think Fiona's place was up here.'

'It isn't, but Fern Barclay's cottage is and I thought Eve might be interested in seeing that too. Well, just the outside, that is.' As they drove along the pleasant residential street, Eve noted the bright gardens and mixture of architectural styles in the houses, many of them weatherboard and painted in bright colours. They were all, she noted, what she would have called 'bungalows'. She commented on this.

'Well, yes, we just call them houses — a two-storey house we usually call that, to distinguish it.' Chloe slowed up and pointed out an attractive yellow-washed stone house on the opposite side of the road. There was a drive at the side of it and a wicket gate to the front garden opening on to a path that led to a front veranda with intricate iron work and a front door with coloured glass above it.

'Oh, but it is lovely!' Eve exclaimed. 'I would love to see inside.' But the empty carport suggested no one was home.

'How big are the farms round here?' she wondered aloud as they drove into the countryside between large fields.

'Mostly in the thousands of acres,' Bill replied. 'You need a good acreage here to make a decent living. It can be hot and dry; Christmas is only the beginning of the summer. We still have January and February to get through and can only hope for good rains in the autumn.'

As he spoke, Chloe turned the car in through a drive gate and drew it up outside a large weatherboard homestead shaded by a stand of magnificent gum trees. Sheep grazed in the paddocks round the house.

'Does Fiona farm?' Adam asked disbelievingly.

'No!' Chloe laughed. 'They let the land off to a neighbour.'

'I see.' Eve thought he sounded relieved.

As they stepped out of the car, the front door opened and a small white poodle erupted, yipping excitedly at them. He was followed only a fraction more soberly by a laughing girl dressed casually in cut-off jeans and an open-necked shirt. She looked so young that Eve found it hard to believe that this was the successful and well-known artiste she had spent most of yesterday afternoon listening to. She suddenly felt old, dowdy and almost as if she were here as a voyeur, and suddenly very much on her own, for Chloe and Fiona were greeting one another excitedly, while Adam helped Bill out of the car and handed him his crutches. To cover her confusion, she bent down and stroked the excited little dog, who was dancing round her on his hind legs.

'You look as if you have been in the wars — how did that happen?' Eve looked up at the strange male voice to see a man had also come out of the house and was looking past her to Bill. For a moment she felt she must be invisible to all but the dog.

6

Fiona broke away from Chloe and hurried forward. 'Beau — come here!' She called the poodle who took not the slightest bit of notice. 'I am so sorry,' she said, smiling warmly at Eve. 'Don't let him be a nuisance to you. I am Fiona, by the way, and this is my brother, Alex.' She waved an airy hand in the direction of the man. 'You are from England?' Chloe, realizing no one had introduced either Eve or Adam properly, looked to her father but he was talking to Alex.

'Yes, this is Eve — she is visiting Australia and spent Christmas with us.' Eve noticed she made no mention of the fact that she was there on her father's invitation. 'And this is Adam.' Chloe nodded casually in his direction.

Fiona burst out laughing. 'I'm sorry but it just sounds too good to be true! Adam and Eve!' She sobered quickly. 'Come on in — I have coffee on the hob.' She embraced them all with her warm smile and led the way into the house. 'I have an American friend whose favourite expression when she takes to a person is, 'There will always be coffee on the hob for you at my house.''

Eve smiled. 'I must remember that one.'

Fiona led the way into the kitchen. 'See — I really do.' She pointed to a shining copper percolator bubbling gently on the stove and greeting them with a heady waft of coffee.

Eve thought she had stepped into a magazine picture of a dream kitchen; its deceptive simplicity proclaimed a master hand in the design and no expense spared in its creation.

'You like it?' Fiona asked as she laid out mugs, sugar, cream and shortbread biscuits on a tray. 'I had Fern Barclay design it; she has a great reputation here in Victoria. I was lucky to get her; she is very busy.'

'Yes, Chloe told me. I had just read an article by her so I am thrilled to see her work in the flesh.'

'Come into the lounge and I'll show you some before and after photos,' Fiona invited as she picked up the tray.

'Are you enjoying your visit to Australia?' Alex asked Eve as he handed her coffee.

'Very much, thanks.'

'Is this just a visit or are you planning on staying here?'

'Oh no, I mean, yes — that is, I'm just here

on a visit,' Eve stammered, thrown off-balance not only by Alex's question but his way of giving more than one hundred per cent attention to the person he was speaking to.

'Have you another tour planned, Fiona?' Chloe's question shifted attention away from her.

'Yes. I expected a good spell at home after my trip to the States but this is New South Wales and Queensland, so Beau can come with me.' She smiled and rumpled the little dog's tight curls; he had jumped up to sit by her, looking for a piece of shortbread. He was not disappointed.

'Are you going too?' Bill asked Alex.

He shook his head. 'Not at the beginning. I have the proofs of my book to correct; I may give myself a break and join Fiona later on. Depends if I can get away from my practice in Melbourne.'

'Are you a doctor?' Adam asked.

Alex shook his head. 'I am a psychologist.'

Those piercing eyes must stand him in good stead; the thought flitted through Eve's mind even before Fiona put in with a throaty giggle, 'Hypnotism is his thing so watch out!'

Alex shot a look of malevolent anger at his sister. Eve smiled to herself; he obviously took himself and his work very seriously and expected others to do so. 'You promised to show me some 'before' photos,' Eve reminded Fiona.

'So I did!' She jumped to her feet and pulled an album from a drawer. She was about to pass it to Eve but changed her mind and held it close to her chest instead. 'Come with me and take the Grand Tour first,' she suggested eagerly. 'Then look at the before photos. You will get a better idea of what Fern achieved.'

Eve jumped eagerly to her feet, coffee forgotten, and followed Fiona from the room. Everything — colour schemes, furnishings, drapes — seemed so right that it was hard to imagine the house had not always looked as it did now. 'Do you live here all the time?' Eve asked as they stood at the window of the last room, Alex's study.

Fiona sighed. 'If only . . . officially we live in Melbourne, but this to me is home. Coming here was sheer bliss after the US tour. Though in all honesty I enjoyed that too!'

'I can imagine.' Eve smiled. How deliciously unspoiled Fiona was; it was hard to believe she was such a celebrity. When they returned to the lounge and Fiona showed her the photos taken before work started, Eve could see why Fern Barclay was considered a top interior designer.

Alex jumped up to answer the phone as she was expressing this view. When he held out the receiver to Fiona with a laconic, 'Fern for you, Fiona. She seems to be having some sort of a problem and thinks you might help,' she felt a sense of suspended reality. It was almost as if thoughts of Fern had conjured her up.

'I can't think of anyone at the moment but I'll see what I can do. If the worst comes to the worst . . . ' Fiona sounded soothing. 'Alex can come and feed Boss.'

Alex shook his head violently but Fiona ignored him. 'I'll be in touch,' she told Fern as she hung up.

'No, I will not go every day and feed that bloody cat!' Alex's furious outburst answered Eve's unspoken question. 'You had no business telling her I would.'

Fiona ignored him and turned to Eve. 'Boss is Fern's cat — she had arranged to let someone have her cottage rent-free for a couple of weeks while she was away, on condition they looked after him.'

Alex's mouth twisted sardonically. 'Lucky for her she can afford such a quixotic action; anyone else would park the creature in a boarding establishment and let the cottage for a good rent.'

'Lucky for Boss too, I would say,' Eve

murmured; she liked cats and would probably have done the same. With that thought, an idea began to form in her mind. 'What an odd coincidence that Fern should ring up just when we were talking about her,' she said as Fiona sat down by her and picked up the album full of before photos again, but interested as she was Eve found it hard to keep her attention on Fern Barclay's work. A cat called Boss had it instead.

Fiona laughed. 'Oh, no, Eve. There is no such thing as a coincidence, or so Alex would claim. My brother believes everything, however slight, happens for a reason.'

'But of course it does.' Alex had been listening to their conversation in addition to conducting one of his own. 'There is order in the Universe.'

Bill, looking sceptical, shuffled to the edge of his seat and reached for his crutches.

'If no one minds I think we should be moving on.' He looked questioningly round the group, his gaze coming to rest on Eve as if she were the one to make the decision. Feeling confused, she jumped to her feet.

'Yes, of course,' she mumbled, fearful of outstaying her welcome although she was enjoying both the company and the surrounds so much she was in no hurry to leave. Adam followed her lead and moved to help

Bill with his crutches. Their movement alerted Beau, who jumped to the ground from his place on the sofa and began dancing on his hind legs and yipping with excitement.

In the flurry of thanks and farewells and settling Bill into the car, the crazy thought that had half-formed in Eve's mind slid into oblivion.

'What now?' Chloe asked as she turned out of the drive gate. 'It is about lunchtime but where shall we head?'

'Back into Elmore?' Bill suggested. 'The Victoria is a decent enough pub.'

It was, Eve agreed, a decent enough pub and they were soon seated at the four sides of a table in the window. Eve found herself looking out into the street with Chloe on one side of her, Bill on the other and Adam across the table from her. Each of them had a glass of cold beer in front of them and as she took a long sip Eve glanced up with a sigh of appreciation and found herself meeting Adam's gaze. For a moment their glances held before Eve felt, rather than saw, that both Chloe and her father were watching them. She hastily transferred her focus to a building on the opposite side of the road. 'What is that place across there?' she asked, more for something to say than because she really needed to know.

Chloe craned her neck to see what held Eve's attention.

'Oh, that's the Campaspe Run — it's a sort of country living museum.'

'Isn't the Campaspe the river that runs through your property?' Adam asked, surprising them all by his question and his apparent knowledge of the countryside.

'Yes, it is — but how did you know?' Chloe asked sharply, sounding, Eve thought, far from pleased.

'I looked at the map.' Both Chloe and her father seemed surprised at the succinctness of his reply. Eve smiled to herself.

'If the Campaspe Run is open we will go and have a look through it — that is, if you would like to?' Bill spoke directly to Eve. 'With your farming background you would find it interesting, I think.'

'Yes, I would — thank you.' Eve accepted as laden plates appeared and were placed in front of them. She bit off the comment that she had escaped from her farming background as soon as she could.

* * *

Once outside the museum, Bill changed his mind.

'I don't feel like hobbling round on these

things.' Bill indicated his crutches with a disgusted face. 'I'll sit out here in the sun and watch the world go by.'

'But ... ' Eve began, suppressing a momentary irritation with Bill who, after all, had been the one to suggest they visit the museum and was now opting out. With a shrug, she followed the other two.

Finding it more interesting than she had expected, Eve took her time and the other two were soon ahead of her. The earlier settlers had brought with them many ideas and customs from the old country, and to her surprise she began to feel nostalgic about her farm childhood. When she caught a glimpse of Chloe and Adam they both, she thought, looked bored, but whether with each other or the museum she was unsure.

'We will go back a different way,' Chloe told them as they settled in the car once more. 'Unless anyone is anxious to get home?'

'Are you going through Axedale?' Bill asked as they turned off the highway on to one of the minor side roads.

'I thought Eve would like to see the gallery.'

'Gallery?' Adam had already noted that Axedale was a very small dot on the map.

'Yep,' was all Chloe said, but Bill turned his head to Eve.

'I think you will like it, Eve, it's a bit of real Australiana.'

Eve did like it, and even Adam was intrigued by the paintings, some covering half a wall, of life in the country a few generations back. Almost all of them were dominated by horses, many of them splendid Clydesdale draught animals. Eve bought a small painting of a team splashing through a ford; the impression of movement and action delighted her.

'Well, did you enjoy your day?' Bill asked later that evening as they lingered over coffee.

'Very much.' She grinned mischievously. 'So much culture. A singer, a painter, a museum and a gallery — all in a day.'

'Not to mention viewing the work of a well-known interior designer and meeting an author,' Chloe added. In response to Eve's puzzlement she explained, 'Alex writes books — on psychology.'

'How interesting. What about?'

'His books are absolute rubbish,' Bill said dismissively. 'Mostly about past lives and how he hypnotizes people back into them — or thinks he does.'

'Maybe he is right, Dad,' Chloe told him.

'Maybe he is,' Adam murmured in a voice

almost too low to hear. Eve decided to keep her own counsel. Reincarnation was a subject she knew little about but she had an open mind on the subject.

'Haven't you ever been somewhere and known you have been there before — even though you haven't?' Adam asked the question in a general way but his eyes rested on Eve. She found herself shaking her head.

'I can't say I have — but I have had that odd feeling that what is happening has happened before. It has a special name — what is it?'

'Déjà vu,' Adam supplied.

Eve nodded. 'Yes.'

'This conversation is getting maudlin,' Chloe protested; Eve judged by the expression on Bill's face that he agreed. What a pity, thought Eve; both the conversation and Adam were promising interest. 'What are we all going to do tomorrow?' Chloe added, looking expectantly at her father and the two guests.

'I don't know what you and Adam are planning, Chloe, but I am taking Eve out for the day.' Bill turned to Eve. 'You have a current driver's licence?'

Eve nodded, too surprised to speak. 'An English one.'

'Good. So long as I don't have to drive I

can manage tolerably well now.'

Eve made the excuse that if she were to be chauffeur the next day she needed an early night. It had been a full day — and tomorrow promised to be another. She had plenty to occupy her thoughts without the insidious and, she told herself, absurd notion that had come to her earlier in the day and kept returning. She read for a while then, taking her own advice, put the book to one side and switched off the bedside light.

It was a full moon or very near it, she guessed, by the brilliance of the light coming through the broad chink in the curtains. Although there was a small fan in the room it still seemed stiflingly hot. Eve pushed back the sheet and padded over to the window to draw the drapes closer together. She noted how beautiful everything looked in the moonlight and was about to turn away when she saw the figure of a man by the far gate. Adam. Feeling the slightly cooler night air touch her hot skin, she was tempted to join him. But with the thought she saw Chloe run lightly down the steps of the veranda and across the yard.

With her hands on the curtains to draw them together, Eve hesitated when she saw them move not closer but further apart. They were quarrelling! Then Adam's hand reached

114

towards Chloe. Was he hitting her? No — he pulled her towards him and bent his head to hers. Eve snatched the curtains shut with a jerk and turned back to bed. As she pulled the light sheet up, she wondered why the scene she had just witnessed disturbed her.

Eve was still grappling with her own emotions when she dropped off to sleep. She was looking forward to tomorrow's outing and the chance to get to know Bill better. She wished she had a clearer idea of his feelings for her, even more of her own feelings. She thought she had just been seizing a wonderful opportunity to visit Australia when she came out here — and yet . . .

7

'I thought we would go to Daylesford,' Bill said to Eve at breakfast but he cast an enquiring look at Chloe as if seeking her approval.

Eve smiled at Bill. 'I will leave it to you to choose.' It seemed he already had. 'As I don't know anything about anywhere here . . . ' Her voice petered out as she realized that her opinion had not been sought.

Chloe reached for the cereal packet. 'Good idea, though it may be busy at this time of the year.' She addressed herself to Eve. 'It is an old spa town, popular in the eighties. It has all been restored as well as the baths in nearby Hepburn Springs. It has natural mineral water, good hotels and shops. Being higher and further south than here it is nearly always green there and several degrees cooler.'

Eve was glad to hear that. Yet another example of the upside-down nature of Australia, she reflected. South was cooler, north hotter.

'Keep on this road till we get into Goornong then turn left on to the highway and head for Bendigo, then straight through the city,' Bill directed as, cautiously, Eve turned the unfamiliar car out of the drive gate.

'I have to drive straight through the city?'

'Simple enough — you just stay on this road and drive straight through. There are about a dozen sets of traffic lights but you just stay on this road.'

It took them about forty minutes, thanks to Eve's careful and slow driving, but by the time they reached the outer suburbs she was feeling more confident. Bill, whatever his private thoughts, made no derogatory comments on her driving.

With Bendigo behind them, Eve felt able to take note of the surrounding countryside, which was already quite different. She noticed the stands at the side of the road selling fruit. 'This is Harcourt; they grow apples round here,' Bill told her. 'We will be in Castlemaine in a minute. How about a coffee break?' He didn't wait for an answer but went on, 'It was planned in the early settlement days to be the same size as Bendigo but it got left behind.' That, Eve supposed, explained the large and imposing post office and other buildings. Bill directed her to a parking spot outside a café with outdoor tables. 'It's a long open stretch once we leave Castlemaine before we get to Daylesford.'

Sipping her coffee, Eve felt relaxed and comfortable in Bill's company; she liked the little town and for a moment felt as if she really belonged. When Bill, who had been watching her closely, reached across the table and touched her hand, she smiled at him.

'Do you think you could ever make your home in Australia?' His words and the touch of his hand on hers focused her thoughts.

'I — I hadn't really thought about it,' she mumbled, but did not draw her hand back for several moments. Looking up, she met his eyes smiling into hers and, flustered, pushed at her empty cup and looked round for her handbag.

'Yes — we had better keep going,' Bill said, as he pushed himself up awkwardly from his seat and reached for his crutches.

As they settled in the car and she groped for her seatbelt, Eve inadvertently leaned into him. For so long he had been someone she 'talked' to on the Internet, not really a flesh-and-blood person. The brief accidental contact changed that; it also made her acutely aware of his maleness.

'It would, I expect, depend as much on what you felt there was in England to go back to as to what you found here?'

'Sorry, I . . . ' Eve, trying to gather her thoughts into some order, realized that Bill was merely continuing their conversation and that a space of only minutes had elapsed since he had asked her if she would ever consider a life in Australia. 'Yes — yes, it would, of course,' she stammered.

'I got the impression that you felt there was not a lot left for you in England.'

'Oh, I wouldn't quite say that.' Eve protested, frantically trying to remember just what she had said in those months of written messages flying between them across the world.

'The lights are red,' Bill warned. Eve decided to give her whole attention to driving for the moment.

There was, as he had said earlier, little other than the small hamlet of Guildford between Castlemaine and Daylesford. 'I like this open country — the feeling of space,' Eve told him. 'This is how we imagine Australia.'

'Plus, of course, kangaroos hopping about all over the place,' Bill teased.

'Well, yes, that as well and a koala up every gum tree. So far I have seen neither. The country changes with every mile.' Eve was taking advantage of the quiet road to admire the scenery. She was loath to admit that he had been more or less right about her ideas of the country.

'Oh, conkers — that takes me back to my childhood!' Eve exclaimed a short while later as they passed a long line of chestnut trees on the approach to Daylesford. They parked the car in the town centre.

'Did you enjoy your childhood on a farm? You obviously learned about cows, not like poor Adam.' Bill asked over lunch.

'I would probably have been just as stupid if I hadn't been born a farm girl,' Eve told him.

'Lucky for Chloe you were . . . '

Eve leaned back in her chair with a sigh and smiled at Bill as she picked up her spoon to stir the caffé latte that had just been put in front of her. 'That was a beautiful lunch. Thank you.'

'I can remember the time when you were pushed to find a decent salad roll in this town,' he reflected, stirring his own coffee. 'Then they restored the baths and everything began to happen; now it is a Mecca for people who enjoy the good things in life.' He paused and looked at her. 'You were going to tell me about your childhood,' he reminded her.

'I was?' Eve hadn't remembered promising anything of the sort but she felt relaxed and mellow after their delicious lunch. 'There is very little to tell. Looking back it didn't seem to last long but at the time . . . '

'It seemed to go on for ever.' Bill filled in the pause.

'Yes, it did. I suppose time goes more slowly for all of us when we are young, especially the bad parts,' Eve said thoughtfully, and once more Bill picked up where she paused.

'And the older you get the more everything speeds up until you reach my age and life is racing by all too fast.'

'You are not that old!' Eve protested, smiling at him as she sipped her coffee.

He shrugged. 'Tell me what was so bad about your childhood.'

'I didn't say it was so bad,' Eve protested. 'It was just that when my mother died suddenly when I was sixteen I had to grow up very fast.'

'That must have been tough,' Bill sympathized. 'You didn't tell me about that in our chats over the Internet.'

'There didn't seem much to tell.' It was Eve now who shrugged as if dismissing the subject. 'Nothing very dramatic happened, my father was a small farmer and had relied on Mum to do so much, not just the house and the garden but the poultry and dairy, plus doing most of the paperwork. I don't think either of us realized how much she did until she wasn't there to do it any more. She helped him milk night and morning then had all the equipment to wash afterwards. I helped sometimes, weekends and holidays, but I wasn't really very willing; I felt bad about it afterwards and when she got really sick I did try to do more. But I had my own dreams, then . . . ' Her voice dropped almost to a whisper. 'Then Mum died and because I was school-leaving age Dad just kept me home to do her work. So much for my dreams. He was pretty strict too — no boyfriends. He probably thought I would be off and leave him. But he did pay me — pocket money, really — and since I had nothing to spend it on I saved it till I had enough to go to night school and do a secretarial course. When I finished that I plucked up courage and took a job in an office. I still lived at home and Dad still found plenty for me to do, then Mavis came on the scene. She was as different from Mum as chalk from cheese. She was a barmaid when he met her, and tough. Mavis knew how to look after herself — she made it clear straight off that she wasn't going to slave away in a cowshed all day. She encouraged me to get a job away from home, not that I needed much encouragement. She and I got on all right, but I don't suppose anyone would want a teenage girl around when they were newly married. But I wasn't prepared for Dad's reaction. He told me that if I went, that was it — there was to be no crawling back if things didn't work out for me. I felt really hurt at the time; took a job in another district and never saw Dad again. About six months later he dropped dead with a heart attack. Mavis inherited the farm, which she promptly sold, and less than a year later I heard she was married. By that time I was married myself. In the best romantic novel style, I married my boss. It certainly seemed very romantic at the time; I was still only nineteen when my daughter was born. By that time I was well and truly grown up!' she finished with a wry smile. 'For a long time after Dad died I felt bad — guilty, I suppose.'

'Thanks for filling me in,' was the only comment Bill made. 'But then you married?'

'Yeah . . . Out of the frying pan into the fire but that is another story altogether and I am sure you have heard enough about me for one day.' She was beginning to feel as if she was being grilled and she wasn't at all sure she liked it. She smiled at him across the table, bent to pick up her handbag and pushed her chair back. 'If you don't mind I am going to the Ladies',' she told him.

He didn't ask any more about her past for the rest of the day but Eve felt it was only a temporary reprieve and it was with some relief that she heard a soft snore as they headed back up the highway from Castlemaine to Bendigo. Confident that she could find the way back without disturbing him, she settled down to enjoy the feeling of freedom that driving gave her. I should get a car, she thought, and then reminded herself that she was only here on a visit, not permanently. 'I should have thought you would have felt angry rather than guilty.' Bill's voice startled her, lost in her own thoughts, she hadn't realized he was awake.

'Angry? What about?'

'If your father hadn't married again you would have inherited the farm.'

'I suppose I would. I hadn't really considered that — I just thought it was all my fault he was dead.'

'Why yours and not — what was her name? The new wife?'

'Mavis,' Eve answered automatically.

'You said she wouldn't do all the work you and your mother had done so probably your father was working far too hard.' He nearly added, 'On top of all the stresses and excitement of a new young wife,' but thought better of it. The idea of asking her to stay had been there in his mind ever since she said she was coming out to Australia and had grown since she arrived and he got to know her. When she told him she was a widow and a grandmother, he hadn't expected someone so youthful in both appearance and manner. He could visualize a pleasant future ahead if she would agree to stay. But he didn't want to rush things, for either of their sakes; although he suspected that she might well have had a similar hope to come all this way.

'I am flattered that you managed to sleep,' Eve said lightly.

'I have no alternative but to trust other people's driving while this damn ankle is plastered up like this,' he admitted. Then realizing that he sounded surly at best, unflattering to her at worst, he added, 'But you are a good driver.'

'I am glad you drive on the same side of the road as we do in England. You probably wouldn't have been able to sleep otherwise,' Eve admitted.

Adam was slumped in an easy chair watching the evening news on TV when they got back. He flicked the mute button on the remote control when they came in. 'Chloe is doing things outside. Shutting up the hens or something,' he told them, adding, rather

125

belatedly, 'Did you have a good day?'

'Very, thanks — and you?' Eve responded, noting that Bill had hobbled off to his own room.

Adam shrugged. 'So-so . . . I am afraid I don't seem to be flavour of the month.' There was a pause that Eve tried to fill but she was unable to find the right words as in her heart she had to agree with him. He grinned mischievously. 'I guess I started off on the wrong foot, or more precisely in the wrong bed!'

'I think we should forget that.' Eve tried to sound serious but she could not help smiling back. As the memory of that crazy, embarrassing incident surged back, her smile broke forth as a full-throated laugh. Adam joined in. They were still laughing when Chloe returned to the house.

'Is the joke worth sharing?' Her voice was cool as she stood in the doorway with a milk bucket in one hand and a bowl of eggs in the other. Eve met Adam's eyes and a silent message flew between them not to mention that unfortunate incident. 'I was just telling Eve that I will probably have to leave tomorrow.'

'Oh!' Eve surprised herself by feeling sorry.

Chloe, on the other hand, merely shrugged. 'Oh — do you have to go?'

8

'Go? Who is going?' Bill appeared in the doorway, leaning heavily on his crutches and looking anxiously at Eve.

'Me.' Adam caught the look of relief that flitted briefly across Bill's face. He glanced at Eve and was mollified to see that she, at least, appeared to be sorry he was going. In spite of their unorthodox meeting, or because of it, he felt more drawn to her than anyone else he had met this Christmas. For the briefest of moments he wished she were leaving with him.

Eve was not entirely surprised that Adam was cutting short his visit. From the very first moment when he climbed into her bed, he had lurched from one minor disaster to another. She had felt for him and thought Chloe could have shown more understanding; he was, after all, her guest.

Too hot to sleep and with a brilliant moon lighting up her bedroom, Eve wondered if she too might be outstaying her welcome. In spite of their long Internet friendship, the fact that Bill had not even told Chloe of her existence, let alone her imminent arrival, stung. Bill probably believed she had come with marriage on her mind, but Australia was somewhere she had always had a yen to visit. That Bill had suggested it just when she had the means was coincidental and fortuitous. Would it be so difficult to stay in this pleasant place with a man as nice as Bill whom she felt she knew well from their months of cyber correspondence? Did it matter that he hadn't lit any inner fires? Wasn't she too old and world-weary — marriage-weary anyway — to imagine her heart going zing, as if she were a love-lorn teenager? In spite of her sensible self-talk, just before she dropped to sleep she remembered the moment when she had carelessly leaned against him — she had been very conscious of his maleness then.

Eve woke suddenly about half an hour later; she could hear a faint rustling and froze in bed. Was there a mouse in the room — or worse, a rat — or even worse, a snake? For a while she lay quite still, literally frozen with terror, remembering the story someone had told with much relish and amusement on Christmas Day, about one of their neighbours who, on hearing such a sound in the night, had got up to investigate and discovered a snake in the wardrobe.

An absurd story, she told herself, just a typical example of the Aussie pleasure in a good story from a storyteller with not too great a respect for the truth and full of Christmas cheer.

She tried to sleep but the whine of a persistent mosquito unpleasantly close to her ear kept her awake. She tried pulling the bedclothes over her head but that threatened death by suffocation so she uncovered her head again, hoping it had gone — a forlorn hope. She sat up and switched on the light and, looking round the room, saw it resting on the wall just above the head of the bed, obviously recouping its resources before renewing the attack. She grabbed a slipper, which she slapped furiously on the wall. It had disappeared — she must have got it. On that comforting thought she settled down again to sleep, only to hear that persistent shrill whine near her ear again just as she thought she might drop off. After another chase with the slipper in which she was almost sure she had been successful, she felt too wide awake to contemplate sleep and, propping her pillows up, reached for her book. It was then that she saw the folded paper pushed under the door. Could that be the 'mouse' that had disturbed her? But who on earth would be writing notes at this time of night and pushing them under her bedroom door?

Eve unfolded the single sheet of paper torn from a notebook. 'This is my mobile number . . . ' she read, and after the list of digits, 'should you need a friend in Australia. Adam.' Her first reaction was annoyance: why should he imagine that she would need a friend, other than those she already had, and anyway, assuming she did, why should she call on him? Then common sense, and caution, or a blend of the two, stopped her screwing up the paper and throwing it away and instead she flattened it out and was about to put it in her wallet when she decided to add it to the list of numbers she had already installed on her own mobile phone. She could not imagine ever needing it — but, as she was fond of saying to herself, you never knew.

She climbed back into bed more wakeful than ever. Why on earth should Adam think she might need his number? In spite of their unorthodox introduction to each other, there had never been anything between them other than sympathetic understanding on her part.

Eve woke to the sound of a car starting up outside. She jumped out of bed and ran to the window, noting that she had slept late. Adam's car was turning out of the gate. A few moments later Chloe called, 'Are you awake? Breakfast is ready,' outside her door.

'Adam had his early, he wanted to get off,'

she explained when Eve, anxious not to annoy her hostess, appeared a few seconds later without bothering to dress.

'Yes — I saw him leave. Hope you don't mind me like this?' Eve indicated her short pyjamas and light robe.

'Dad isn't up yet,' was Chloe's enigmatic reply. Eve, knotting the sash of her robe round her waist, translated that as '*So long as Dad doesn't see you like that.*' 'No doubt you were both tired after your day out yesterday,' she added.

'Did Adam have a special reason to leave? I mean . . . ' Eve stammered. 'I thought he was staying for a fairly long visit.' Trying to repair what sounded a singularly tactless remark she added, 'I mean, did he get sent for or something?' She felt she was making things worse so concentrated on her breakfast and willed her tongue to keep still.

'No,' Chloe all but snapped. 'He just came for Christmas. I asked him on impulse, or under the influence of too much party spirit.' She smiled wryly. 'He probably accepted for the same reason.' Not knowing how to respond, Eve mumbled vaguely and was startled when Chloe added, 'I hope you aren't thinking of rushing off?' As Eve had been thinking of exactly that, she looked up in surprise. Were her thoughts so transparent?

'Dad seemed to enjoy himself yesterday,' Chloe added.

'So did I,' Eve was quick to assure her. She sipped her coffee slowly, feeling faintly uncomfortable, guilty almost, as if she were being questioned.

'You and Dad seem to be getting on well together.' There it was again; an innocent enough remark that nevertheless seemed to carry hidden meaning.

'Yes, we do.' Eve looked the younger woman straight in the eyes. If she was fishing for information, she would not get it from her. 'I had better get dressed.'

When she returned to the kitchen dressed casually in shorts and a cool shirt, Eve found Bill by himself, looking helpless in the manner perfected by the male sex to extract help from women. As she offered to cook him breakfast, Eve reflected that women probably did the same when there was a man job to be done.

'Bacon and eggs?' Bill suggested tentatively. Eve smiled her assent.

She had just put the plate down in front of him and was dropping bread in the toaster when Chloe walked in.

'Has that boyfriend of yours left already?' Bill asked.

'He left before you were up,' Chloe

snapped, 'and he is not, never was, my boyfriend.'

'So you say,' Bill answered disbelievingly, 'but I doubt if he would agree with you.' He reached for the salt and pepper and shook both liberally over his eggs. 'I can't say I'm sorry to see him go; couldn't take to the fellow myself.'

'Lucky you didn't have to, then, wasn't it, Dad?' Chloe rapped back. Eve started to murmur vaguely that he had seemed quite nice to her but the words died on her lips at the sight of Chloe's thunderous expression. Eve couldn't resist a soothing, 'Cheer up — it may never happen.' Then she added, 'You look as if you have lost a dollar and found ten cents.'

Chloe snarled, 'What on earth is that supposed to mean?'

'That you look bad-tempered,' Bill told his daughter. 'That's right, isn't it, Eve?'

Chloe ignored this, merely saying sourly to her father, 'It is a pity you weren't a better correspondent, Dad. Kept me up to date with the local news a bit — it might have saved some trouble.' He looked blankly at Eve, who had seen her reaction on Christmas Day when Maureen and Gary announced they were getting married. She found her irritation turn to sympathy.

For a while the only sound was Bill munching toast. Lost in her thoughts, Eve jumped when the phone rang. Chloe snatched it off its rest, glanced swiftly at Eve then walked with it out on to the veranda pulling the door partially shut behind her. Eve heard her say, 'I don't know whether she will . . . ' before she walked further along the veranda out of earshot and Bill began to speak. She was certain the 'she' referred to was herself but couldn't guess at the context or even who the caller was. She thought she must have been wrong when Chloe came in to return the phone to its rest and, looking directly at her father, said, 'Steve wants me to help him muster their sheep.'

Eve was about to volunteer her own help, imagining that a day or a morning on horseback doing a useful job of work would be interesting, when Chloe added, 'I am sure you will be able to entertain your guest, won't you, Dad?'

Eve caught her breath in a small gasp which, in an attempt to hide her disappointment, she exhaled in a sigh. Chloe had spoken so decisively it had almost been a snub.

'You would probably have liked to have gone with her?' Bill said when Chloe had gone.

Eve wondered if Bill wished Chloe had invited her; maybe after spending the previous day in her company he would have liked a quiet day on his own.

'No — no, of course not.' She got up and took their dishes to the sink and began to wash up.

'Do you particularly want to go out anywhere or will a quiet day at home satisfy you?'

Eve stiffened; surely he could have put the same question more graciously. The way he asked made her sound like an encumbrance. Perhaps like Adam, she too was an unwanted guest.

'I am quite happy staying here. Please don't feel you have to entertain me.' Her smile was over-bright as she looked at him over the tea towel in her hands.

'Where are you going?' He hadn't meant to sound so sharp.

'Just to my room.'

She pulled the bedding together then dropped down on the freshly made bed and grabbed a magazine, so determined not to wonder what had happened to the comfortable relationship that had developed between them the day before that she failed to notice it was upside-down.

Poor Bill, he must feel so frustrated, unable

to participate in the life of the farm going on around him, and a visitor in the house as well. No wonder he was cranky. She threw aside the magazine and went back to the kitchen.

His tentative smile was shamefaced. 'I am being an old grouch,' he admitted. 'Of course we will go out somewhere . . . You won't want to waste a whole day of your holiday stuck here.'

'I'm quite happy here,' Eve assured him, wondering why he felt it necessary to stress that she was just a visitor. 'You can tell me about the life here, about the farm . . . ' She floundered. 'You know what I mean — tell me about everyday life here.' Her voice petered out. She sounded more as if she were interviewing him with a view to deciding whether or not to stay here, and this when he had just made it clear she was a temporary visitor. Obviously he had not, as he thought possible in their on-line acquaintance, liked her enough to raise the possibility of her visit being permanent. The knowledge was depressing, made humiliating by her own foolish babble.

'Shall we sit out on the veranda before it gets too hot?' Bill suggested. Noting that he was getting increasingly adept with his crutches, Eve made no move to help him.

It was still cool outside. Out across the paddocks Eve could see a flight of birds flying up, wheeling round and then up again. She wondered how they avoided catastrophic mid-air collisions. As they flew closer she caught a glimpse of their rose-pink undersides. They wheeled again and flew off, just a flock of grey birds flying aimlessly. Yet she felt they knew exactly where they were going — and why. She wished she could say the same for herself.

9

Bill followed her gaze. 'We call people 'silly galahs' or say they are behaving like a galah,' he commented. 'Unjust. They are not stupid. Pests, maybe, when they raid our crops.'

'I was thinking it nothing short of a miracle they don't fall out of the sky in a series of mid-air crashes.' Eve smiled. She was finding it both pleasant and relaxing sitting here with nothing better to do than watch birds fly. Her life to date had not presented many such opportunities.

'The only good thing about this damn leg is that I have time to just sit and think.' Bill echoed her thoughts.

'I was thinking much the same thing — not about your leg, about myself. I had never realized before how rewarding doing nothing can be, and this is a very pleasant spot to do it.'

'Good enough to consider it as a permanency?'

'What?' Eve was jolted out of her meditative mood. 'I don't know. I — I haven't thought about it.'

Bill turned towards her with raised

eyebrows. Eve felt herself colouring at the expression on his face; he knew she had thought about it.

'Didn't you decide to come out for Christmas and see how you liked it here, and how we got on together when we met in the flesh?' He smiled to himself; that was not a good choice of phrase, given the circumstances, but he ploughed on gamely. 'After all, it is easy enough to strike up a friendship as pen-pals, or in this case cyber friends. It is possible to say anything when you can't actually hear the other person's voice, see their face as they tell you — Well, they could be telling you anything.'

'Is that what you think I have been doing?' It sounded to Eve as if he were accusing her of lying.

'No. Do you think I have?'

She shook her head. 'No — only . . . '

'Only what?'

'Well, Bill, to be honest I can't understand why you didn't tell Chloe about me. It would certainly have made things easier in the first instance. And even now I don't know how she feels about me. One minute I think maybe she likes me just a little. The next, well . . . '

'That was a mistake,' Bill admitted, 'but I wasn't to know that I would be laid up in hospital when you arrived. I probably shouldn't have asked Steve to meet you but I couldn't think of any other way of getting you here.'

'I am afraid Chloe seemed to think I snatched Steve up from somewhere, but as she doesn't seem to want him herself I can't see what she objected to.' She paused, wrinkling her forehead in thought. 'Then of course there was that embarrassing episode with Adam.'

'But there is nothing between Chloe and Steve, more's the pity. I wish there was but their relationship hasn't moved on from their childhood days. She looks on him as a brother. But it isn't my daughter I want to discuss at the moment, Eve, it is you — or rather you and me.'

Eve waited for him to continue; it seemed an aeon before he spoke again and when he did she was taken by surprise at his words.

'I don't think either of us has turned out to be quite what we expected, have we, Eve?'

'I — I don't know. I am not quite sure what you mean.' She spoke hesitantly. Was he about to tell her that she was a bitter disappointment to him and he wanted her to leave?

'I think I am older than you imagined and you are certainly younger than I expected.'

140

His voice was gentle and he smiled at her as he spoke.

'But I told you my age,' Eve protested. 'Never made any secret of the fact that I was thirty-nine when we met.'

'Ah, yes — the longest ten years of a woman's life, between thirty-nine and forty.'

'Don't you believe me?'

'I believe you — of course I do. Sorry, that was just a feeble joke that slipped out,' Bill immediately apologized.

Eve smiled ruefully. 'Well, it was true then, when we first got to know each other, but I have to come clean and admit I have had a birthday since then and have hit the big four-oh.'

'Am I older than you expected?'

Eve shook her head. 'No. Why so much concern about age?'

'Well, you know what they say. 'A woman is as young as she looks and a man as old as he feels'.'

'So, I look my age. How old do you feel?'

'About ninety-nine with this bloody leg,' he retorted morosely.

'And what about the rest of you?' Eve all but snapped. 'It was bad luck and I feel for you, but it hasn't made you an old man overnight any more than turning forty made me an old woman.'

'You said you were a grandmother, but you don't seem like one.'

'Would you like me to put on my shawl and mob cap?' Eve did not know where all this was leading, other than to the end of their relationship. 'You are annoyed because I am not more grandmotherly?' This seemed to her quite bizarre; most men, surely, were looking for someone younger and more glamorous, not older and more staid. Eve felt a sharp frisson of anger but managed to keep it in check. 'I have never lied to you. I married very young and so did my daughter; I was not quite forty when my grandson was born. I am sorry I have disappointed you with my ungrandmotherly appearance,' she told him and half rose to her feet, intending to escape before her annoyance took over.

'Don't be so touchy. It may not have come out right but I actually meant to be complimentary,' laughed Bill. 'All I wanted to say was that you don't look like a grandmother; I certainly didn't mean to imply I didn't like the way you look — far from it.'

'We are not in the eighteenth century when women were expected to dress in black, wear a mob cap and behave and think old. So what should a grandmother look like?'

'Simmer down.' He made a patting down

gesture with his hand. 'It is not *your* age I am concerned about — it is *mine*.'

Eve thought that was more her concern than his in this context but said nothing. She looked at him in surprise when he asked, 'What about Adam? He is nearer your age.'

'He is thirty-five,' Eve snapped, immediately wishing the words unsaid. Before he could point out that to know his age showed a degree of intimacy, she parried, 'Why this sudden obsession with age, anyway?' She repressed memories of the odd moments when sexual awareness had flared between herself and Adam. But it was not so easy to forget the cryptic note he had left pushed under her door, although she had no intention of mentioning it.

'Adam has left,' she reminded Bill, letting her fingers rest on his arm for a second. 'And as far as age goes, he was five years younger than me, you are five years older. By my reckoning, that is about equal.'

His lop-sided smile gave him a boyish look. 'Maybe,' he suggested, 'it wouldn't be a bad thing if I remembered the pinch of sugar and you took my silly grumbling with a grain of salt.'

Eve looked and felt mystified. His smile widened, creasing the skin round his vivid blue eyes.

'The way for a man and woman to get on is for her to take everything he says with a grain of salt and to add a pinch of sugar to everything she says to him.'

Eve laughed. Any irritation she had felt dissolved. 'I guess that is pretty true,' she agreed, 'though a tad chauvinistic, but if we *both* remember the sugar there should be no problems. I have never heard that before — you have a wonderful fund of these snippets of homespun philosophy.'

He shrugged, dismissing the compliment. 'I still don't understand how someone as young as you came to be a grandmother.'

'I am sure I have told you about Tony.' Eve protested.

'Your husband?' Bill murmured.

Eve shook her head. Briefly she had travelled back in time to that short, all too sweet, period. Nothing had seemed quite real and nothing had prepared her for the turbulence of her feelings. She had persuaded her father to let her do an evening computer course. That was where she met Tony. She told her father the sessions were ending later and went to a milk bar for coffee with Tony. When he suggested she meet him other nights she sneaked out after dark, revelling in the romance of these illicit meetings. Afterwards she knew her blatant adoration of

Tony must have rather bored him, denying him the thrill of the chase. Inevitably the moment came when he demanded more.

'Tony had just got his first car,' she told Bill. 'When he suggested he take me for a spin instead of coffee I thought that was reasonable, but he only went as far as a quiet lane a short distance from my home. He stopped the car in a gateway and kissed me, then he said, 'Get into the back seat — I can't do a thing here with this damn steering wheel in the way, and the gear lever between us.' I did so because it was uncomfortable. That's how naïve I was. When he pulled at my clothes so violently that a button came off my blouse, I begged him to stop, but he held me tighter and kissed me so hard I couldn't yell. He forced his tongue into my mouth. I tried again to yell but I could hardly breathe; the more I tried to get free the tighter he held me.' Eve felt herself grow hot remembering the electrifying feeling when he touched her, so that suddenly not wanting him to stop was stronger than her fear. She was embarrassed, too, realizing that she was telling Bill this. She was silent as she remembered the sudden pain as he forced his way into her and thumped up and down on top of her. She remembered thinking that if this was 'IT' then what the hell was all the fuss about? It had been much more enjoyable when he had just caressed her with his hands. But she said none of this aloud.

'He said he would bring something next time, that I needn't worry about getting pregnant — nobody ever did the first time,' she murmured, then stopped short, remembering that she had worried, and with cause. She looked anxiously at Bill, not quite sure how much she had said aloud, how much had been just remembering. She was relieved to see he didn't look shocked, only angry, and when he muttered 'The bastard!' she knew it was not directed at her.

Eve's voice had been barely audible, then she spoke in a would-be bright voice. 'I think I will tell you the rest another time — that is, if you really want to hear it.'

'I'm sorry,' Bill said gently, taking her hand in his. 'I didn't mean to probe into your past.' He smiled. 'How about a cup of coffee?'

'Good idea, I'll put the jug on.' Reliving that period in her life had been painful, but bottled-up secrets were not a good basis for a relationship.

They were sitting in a companionable silence drinking their coffee when Bill startled her by saying, 'I hope you didn't have to find out the hard way that he was quite wrong in saying that?'

Saying what? she asked herself wildly, then remembered that she had told him that Tony had assured her that no one got pregnant the first time they had sex. 'I am afraid I did,' she said at last.

'Don't look so shattered.' His voice was gentle and he touched her arm lightly with the tips of his fingers, a mere butterfly touch but somehow it gave her comfort and strength. 'You are not the first, and I am sure you will not be the last, to find yourself in that position. Today it seems quite the norm to have one's children acting as bridal attendants at the wedding.' Eve gave a small half-smile and he looked at her keenly. 'Or wasn't there a wedding?'

'Oh, there was a wedding.' Bill would never believe what happened next. Maybe this was the moment when she should smile sweetly and tell him to mind his own business, or maybe that she had decided to return to England. 'How have you got me to reveal the sordid secrets of my past life while you keep mum about yours?' was what she actually said, adding with a wobbly smile, 'Perhaps you don't have any.'

'We all have secrets, things in our past we don't want anyone to know,' he answered quietly. 'I am really sorry if I have forced you to remember things you would rather not; I didn't intend to. I just wondered how you came to be a grandmother so young and who you married.'

Eve almost reminded him that she had said earlier that he would have to wait for the next instalment, but maybe their coffee break was wait enough. What the hell, she said to herself. I might as well tell all and be done with it. 'I — I married his father,' she finally told him.

'His father?' Bill's voice croaked with astonishment. 'But . . . why?'

'By the time I realized I was pregnant, Tony had left for New Zealand to stay for a year on his uncle's sheep station. His father had been a widower for quite a while; he pointed out that he needed a housekeeper and I needed a husband and the child a father. It all seemed quite sensible at the time, and, after all, he was the biological grandfather.

'Marion was born a month after my nineteenth birthday. Oddly, almost from birth she was more Harry's child than mine — 'Daddy's girl', everyone called her. Ironic, really. She had just had her twentieth birthday when Joel, my grandson, was born. She and Hugh appear to live in happy harmony, without the benefit of marriage.'

They sat in silence while Eve grappled with her thoughts.

'I am afraid I lied to you. I'm sorry.' Her voice was low.

'You made all that up?' Bill stared at her.

'No — no. That was all true. I mean earlier — when we first got to know one another on the Net. I told you I am a widow. Not true. I divorced Harry.'

Bill was relieved; for a moment he had thought she was about to say she was still married. He didn't ask himself why it was important that she was not.

'It was nothing dramatic. We had managed to rub along tolerably well over the years, then he re-met his first love.' She shook her head. 'Not Tony's mother — I gather he married her on the rebound after a silly quarrel with Meg. Anyway, when he met her again I decided our marriage wasn't worth hanging on to and agreed to a divorce. Marion was always much more his than mine so I wasn't surprised — hurt a little, maybe, but not surprised — when she blamed me for the break-up. When she eventually chose to live with him it was almost a relief. I was afraid she would make the same mistakes I did, and maybe not be so lucky. It is such a pity our children can't learn from our mistakes — that is the hard part of being a parent, seeing the inability of our children to profit and learn from our mistakes — but I realize now we all have to make our own. The more I lectured the worse things became. Her reaction ranged from wails of, 'Mum, you have no idea,' 'Mum, you just don't understand!' to rows and temper tantrums in which she said — Well, never mind what she said, let's just say it was sometimes so hurtful I just don't want to think about it. At times I wondered why I had bothered — I could have given her up for adoption, even had an abortion, but instead I chose an option that gave her a good home and a father.

'Would you do that today?' Eve, reliving the past and thinking out loud, had almost forgotten her listener. She turned to him now and shook her head. 'No, I would probably do the same again. Marion has no idea that Harry is really her grandfather.'

'Suppose Tony had come back?'

'Then we would have had to face the situation when it happened. But he liked it so much he just stayed on. The last I heard of him he was happily married. He never knew that Marion was his.'

Bill thought that if he had bothered to do his sums he might well have suspected, and that might have had something to do with his decision to stay. Sudden irritation with what seemed to him the selfishness of the people in Eve's life made him speak more sharply than he intended. 'Stop blaming yourself, particularly for your father's death. Guilt is a pointless and very destructive emotion, a self-indulgent luxury — snap out of it, Eve!'

'I am sorry you see me as self-indulgent,' she told him in a voice she tried to keep cool. His words had stung for she saw herself as anything but.

'That is not quite what I said . . . or meant. The trick to living is to get on with things, move forward and forget the guilt.' Bill pushed himself awkwardly and impatiently to his feet. 'I'm afraid I have paperwork that must be done.' With that he made his way back into the house. Eve listened to the sound of his crutches followed by a banging door.

10

Eve sailed across the yard on a wave of righteous indignation but instead of going to the paddocks she walked down the drive with no clear idea of where she was going.

She had no hat, the sun was getting hot and the flies were active, but just as she was about to turn back she saw the mail van stop and an arm appear and drop a bundle of letters into the old cream churn that served as a mail-box. She might as well collect them now she had got this far. She reached inside the dusty, and she hoped not spidery, interior and drew out a thick bundle of letters bound together with an elastic band. She retraced her steps back to the house swatting vainly at a swarm of black flies buzzing round her head. She remembered remarking to Chloe that people always seemed to be waving in Australia, and receiving the laughing rejoinder, 'That's just the Great Aussie Wave. They are not being friendly — most of the time they are swatting at flies.'

She dropped the bundle of letters on the kitchen bench, wondering briefly whether she should hand them to Bill, but decided against it. She strolled over to the bookcase where a new-looking book with a bright cover caught her eye; she pulled it out and read the author's name with a puzzled frown, before remembering that Alex Cameron was Fiona's brother. The psychologist who wrote books, no doubt, she thought with some cynicism, hoping to reach the same dizzy heights as Dr Phil of TV fame. She read the title, *Do You Remember Living Before?* Thank God, no. One life was more than enough for her to cope with. She was about to push it back when the words on the inside flap of the dust jacket caught her attention. '*Are events, people, problems from a past life intruding into this life? Maybe they are the hidden cause of your difficulties. Alex Cameron has hypnotized hundreds of people back into what he believes are previous lives and by getting them to face these hidden memories has helped them sort out present-day difficulties.*'

'Crap!' Eve muttered aloud, then she remembered Alex Cameron's eyes. She didn't doubt his ability as a hypnotist and was sure he was more than competent enough to extract excellent corroborative stories from his victims. Bill had not emerged from his room and his paperwork so she took the book to her own room. She stretched out on the bed and opened it at the first chapter. Her logical brain told her that the whole idea was just one enormous cop-out, an excuse not to be responsible for one's actions. Nevertheless, a tiny part of her brain suggested the possibility that there might be something of interest between the pages.

Although she did not agree with what Alex was saying, she discovered he had a most compelling way of saying it, and the case histories he recorded read like exciting fiction so that she just kept on reading. She was almost halfway through the book when she heard Chloe come back; there were no voices so she must be alone. A glance at her watch shocked her into leaping off the bed; it was almost half-past one, no wonder she was hungry. Mentally cursing Alex, she tossed the book down and went out to the kitchen.

'Oh, there you are. I thought you and Dad would have had lunch by now.'

'I'm sorry.' Chloe's offhand manner made Eve feel guilty. 'I was reading and the time sort of slipped by.'

'It must have been a very engrossing book — what was it?'

'Alex Cameron's book — I borrowed it from the bookcase. Sorry . . . ' There she was, apologizing again.

'Don't be sorry,' Chloe laughed. 'I call that

154

a penance. I couldn't read it — I thought it was the most utter rubbish and very boring at that. But if you got lost in it to the extent you didn't notice it was lunchtime, I guess you don't agree?'

'Well, I do agree that it is a bit far-fetched — I can't say I go along with all that past lives stuff — but he has a wonderful style. Somehow he gets you sucked in and you just go on reading.' Her voice trailed off slightly at the expression on Chloe's face and she almost apologized again. 'I did begin to think there might be something in his theory.'

'Oh yeah — it pays well,' Chloe drawled, slamming cheese and bread on the table. 'I haven't had lunch either; I decided to come home. Where's Dad by the way?'

'He said he had paperwork to do — ' Eve began, but before she could finish they heard his crutches against the floor and he pushed open the door and limped across to the table without speaking. Chloe, busy slicing tomatoes, glanced from one to the other. 'How do, happy campers!'

Eve, pretending not to hear, took the lettuce out of the crisper and arranged it in a bowl. Bill began to look through the pile of letters Eve had collected from the mail-box. Most of the envelopes had windows, she assumed they must be bills and saw his lips tighten.

Chloe looked across at her father then, looking at Eve, she raised her eyebrows and shrugged. 'Come on, Dad.' Her tone was rallying. 'Have lunch and look at those afterwards. They may not seem so bad on a full stomach.'

Bill grunted and muttered, 'Doubt it,' but he did push the pile of envelopes to one side and help himself to food. Chloe looked from one to the other; it seemed obvious to her that whatever had been going on here this morning had not improved the tempers of either of them. Her own morning had been less than satisfactory too. Steve had told her how delighted the whole family was about the engagement of Maureen and Gary. As she was still struggling to come to terms with it, Chloe could not agree and he had asked her sharply if the cat had got her tongue this morning, or had she just got out of bed on the wrong side? Feeling she could not listen to any more rapturizing over the engagement, she had refused lunch and come home to find her father and his guest even more out of sorts with the world in general than she was herself.

'What don't you like about Alex's book?' Eve asked to break the silence.

Chloe chewed thoughtfully on the cheese and tomato sandwich she had made for herself and absently reached for a piece of lettuce. 'I agree with you that he has a great writing style but as far as I was concerned that was the only thing that saved it from being dead boring. Quite honestly he can be a bit of a pill when he talks about it too — he is so hung up on the subject, when he was actually writing that book he was a positive menace. I daren't go near him in case he conned me into being hypnotized!'

'Lucky you weren't home then at the time,' Bill cut in drily.

Chloe looked flustered. 'That's not true, Dad. He had just got the idea of the book and was looking for guinea pigs to experiment on so that he could get plenty of good material when I last saw him.' She turned back to Eve. 'If you enjoyed it write and tell him so — or better still ring him up. He loves to have his ego stroked.'

Eve wondered whether Chloe had an issue with Alex's book or Alex himself, and did not take her suggestion seriously.

'You could have a session with him.' Both women looked at Bill in surprise. Chloe had never heard her father make anything but derogatory remarks about Alex Cameron's 'whacky ideas', so surely he couldn't be serious? But he was not smiling and Eve was flushing as if his words had touched a sore spot.

'Maybe I will. Perhaps I will benefit from it — others seem to have done,' she responded, flashing Bill a defiant glance.

Eve, concentrating on her lunch, could feel the waves of astonishment from both Bill and Chloe, but pride would not let her take back her hasty words.

'Well, if you really mean that I will drive you over — it would be fun to see Fiona again if she is there,' Chloe, recovering first, gabbled in her anxiety to smooth things over.

Eve tried not to look as appalled as she felt at the suggestion.

'If she is not you too can be hypnotized.' Bill's dry voice was dry and humourless.

'Let it drop, Dad,' Chloe said tersely. 'Neither of us intends to be hypnotized. Well, I certainly don't and I don't think Eve does, do you?'

Eve shook her head emphatically. 'No way! I would be interested to talk to him, hear him explain a bit more about just what he does. Most of the book is a rehash of people's experiences under hypnosis.' Her voice faded out; she wanted to hear what Chloe, who was already dialling, said to Alex.

Putting her hand over the mouthpiece, she

turned round and said in a low voice to Eve, 'I know she said she was off on tour round Australia soon but I can't remember when, can . . . ' She turned back to the phone. 'Oh, hi, Alex! Is — is Fiona there? Oh dear . . . I guess we had better come some other time then.' Her voice trailed off and she appeared to be listening carefully to what Alex had to say. 'No — no — it isn't really important . . . it's just that . . . '

Eve held her breath, hoping Chloe wasn't going to bring her into it, and flapped her hand at Chloe in an attempt to stop her. She was without success; Chloe was explaining to Alex, 'Eve has been reading your book and seems rather intrigued . . . ' Oh God, Eve thought, whatever am I letting myself in for? Chloe gushed, 'Terrific! We will come this afternoon.' She replaced the receiver and turned to Eve with a slightly malicious smile of triumph. 'Fiona is away. Alex was quite excited at having a fan visit him.'

'I am not a fan,' Eve said firmly, 'and I don't particularly want to see him; I am only about halfway through the damn book. However, since you seem to have set up a sort of 'meet the author' session, I suppose I had better go. But I warn you — I have no intention whatsoever of being hypnotized.'

'Famous last words,' Bill muttered.

'You'll come, won't you Dad?'

Bill shook his head. 'No, thanks. I'm still grappling with paperwork. I need to get down to it and not keep taking days off to go on trips.'

Eve felt herself flushing; was he deliberately trying to make her feel guilty because he was out with her all day yesterday?

'What time are we starting?' she asked Chloe. As there seemed no way of getting out of it, she might as well make the best of things.

Chloe didn't answer but busied herself clearing away the lunch. Thinking she hadn't heard her, Eve was about to repeat her question when Chloe, still with her back to her, muttered something about Eve driving her car.

'What are you talking about? I don't want to drive — you can drive yourself.'

'No, I meant you go by yourself — it would be much better really. To tell you the truth I am not all that keen on Alex Cameron — if Fiona was at home it would be different. Much better for you to go by yourself. I don't need my car this afternoon. You'll be OK, really you will.'

Eve gaped at her. How on earth had she got herself into this? 'But I don't know the way,' she protested, grasping at straws.

160

'There is a really good road map of the area in the car — and I will write down directions for you as well,' Chloe was quick to assure her.

Eve glared at her own reflection in the mirror as she combed her hair. She wished Bill were coming with her, but after his adamant refusal when Chloe suggested it she was not going to risk a snub by asking him.

'Enjoy yourself — and be good. And if you can't be good — be careful!' Chloe quipped as she proffered the keys and scribbled directions.

Eve's good humour reasserted itself as she drove out of the McMahons' gate. Alex Cameron may be a pretentious egghead who had written a rather silly book but Eve enjoyed driving, and was glad to get away from what seemed a somewhat fraught atmosphere. She pressed a button on the CD player and recognized Fiona's pleasant voice singing a ballad she had already heard. She relaxed, appreciating the straight roads and lack of dense traffic. What a waste of land these huge verges, or nature strips as they called them here, were. She had a good idea of location and found she didn't need the road map; Chloe's directions and her own memory were sufficient. The feeling of freedom was so heady that she thought she might miss her way 'accidentally on purpose', but she would be asked for an account of her visit with Alex. She planned to make her visit as short as possible; perhaps she could find a long way back.

Eve stopped the car in the shade of the stand of eucalypts in front of the Cameron house and took a deep breath before leaving the car. Two men were walking towards her from round the rear of the house. She stared in astonishment. One she recognized as Alex, but what on earth was Adam doing here? Both men raised a hand in greeting; Eve waved back, took another deep breath, and walked towards them.

'I didn't expect to see you here,' she told Adam then, extending her hand to Alex, 'I hope you don't mind me coming?'

'Not at all. I am always pleased to meet my fans.'

Arrogant bastard, Eve thought, but merely smiled. 'Chloe exaggerated. I am reading your book.'

Alex looked slightly put out but recovered when Adam smiled broadly. 'Come in and have a cool drink.' Becoming the urbane host, Alex led the way into the house. In the kitchen they stood expectantly behind him at the fridge, rather, Eve thought, like children.

'Beer or iced lemon?' Alex asked without turning round.

Eve was about to opt for the beer then, remembering that she needed a very clear head, said she would have the lemon.

'Good choice,' Alex said approvingly. 'I can vouch for it. The only ingredients are lemons, water and sugar. Oh, and ice of course — and what is more, the lemons are off our own tree.'

'And you made it yourself,' Adam put in, 'as I can testify having watched you. So pour me a lemon too, please.'

Alex brought out a large jug of lemon drink, added more ice cubes to a bowl and put it along with three glasses on a tray. 'We'll have it on the back veranda,' he told them. 'It is shady and quite pleasant there.'

'I didn't expect to see you here,' Eve said again to Adam as she pulled out one of the wrought iron garden chairs and sat down. 'I thought you had gone back to Sydney — or wherever it was you came from.'

'New Zealand, but I am working in Sydney for the time being.'

'Oh — I see,' Eve murmured, surprised to learn he was not Australian, but still left wondering what he was doing here. As she formed the question in her head, Alex supplied the answer.

'As far as I can gather he only got as far as Elmore when he felt the need for a drink, which is how I came to find him. When I found him he was on his way to nowhere and no pressing need to get there and as he was also a countryman of mine, I suggested he spend some time here.'

'I didn't know you came from New Zealand.'

Eve felt she was expected to make some comment but wished she had remained silent when Alex said with some asperity, 'Why should you? I don't wear a placard announcing it and I have been here so long I have almost forgotten myself. Fiona has spent most of her life here. She and Chloe met at school.' Alex looked at her over the rim of his glass. 'So, you have read my book?'

'Not exactly. That is, I am only about halfway through.'

Alex raised his eyebrows. 'Should I take it as a compliment that you want to see me before you have finished it — or not?'

Eve, unable to think of a polite yet truthful answer, wondered if it would be possible to make her excuses and simply get up and leave.

'I gather the answer is 'Not'. What bothered you?'

Alex's unruffled but somewhat sardonic

courtesy incensed Eve. She gulped down her lemon drink, which she was forced to admit was extremely good, and, determined to leave, tried to push the heavy chair back. It didn't move, so that when she attempted to stand it caught the back of her knees and she sat down again with a bump. 'It didn't 'bother' me, I just thought the whole idea was absurd.'

'You came here to tell me that?' Alex looked astonished.

Adam looked amused.

'No . . . ' Eve began, but stopped short when she couldn't drag up a good reason for coming. 'Well . . . ' she floundered, 'I was reading your book. I found it in the bookcase and I had nothing to do . . . ' Heavens, she was getting in deeper with every word, and both men were looking at her with wry amusement. She took a deep breath and started again. 'I found your book in the bookcase and began reading it. You do have a page-turning style even if I couldn't go along with the content. Chloe suggested I come along and discuss it with you. I thought she intended to come too but when she found Fiona was not here she said she would lend me her car instead — so here I am,' she finished lamely.

'I am so flattered.' Eve looked at Alex

sharply to see if he was being sarcastic. She decided he was. Adam looked from one to the other with quizzical but not unfriendly amusement, and then, suddenly, they were all laughing.

'Aren't you — well — offended?' Eve tentatively asked Alex.

'Should I be?' he parried. 'You certainly wouldn't win any prizes for diplomacy but I do seem to have got under your skin. I have made you feel just a little and perhaps even think a tiny bit, therefore I have been, if only very marginally, successful. I don't really mind whether you agree wholeheartedly with what I say or passionately disagree. I have *moved* you, enough to come and tell me the whole thing is crap.'

'Oh, I didn't say that!' Eve protested. 'It's just that it reads more like some crazy fairy tale than a serious book on psychology. Can you tell me, hand on heart, that you really believe all that guff about reincarnation?'

'Can you tell me you do not?' Alex countered. 'Hasn't it occurred to you that if something is so it does not depend on your belief?'

'No, of course not . . . ' Eve suspected Alex was playing her like a fish on a line; at any moment she was going to trip up on her own words. She managed to rise to her feet, this time without falling childishly back. 'I — I had better go.' She held out her hand formally to Adam. 'I suppose this really is goodbye now.'

Adam shrugged. 'Probably — I think Chloe has seen more than enough of me. We didn't really hit it off; in fact, my visit has been rather a disaster from my arrival to my departure. I hope you and Bill do better.'

Eve didn't think it very likely; he had seemed so cranky when she left, she told Adam.

'Well, you haven't signed a contract or something, have you?' Adam asked lightly. 'We are both lucky not to have got irrevocably tied up. But I am sorry it hasn't worked out for you. I liked Bill, and I know he liked *you*, and at least you didn't have an ex-girlfriend or childhood sweetheart around. Chloe had eyes for no one but Steve. I got a bit fed up with not even coming a poor second.'

'Are you sure?' Eve asked doubtfully.

'Sure she wished she had never asked me? Just about one hundred per cent.'

'No, I didn't really mean that — I was thinking about her and Steve. I can see he is nuts about her but she isn't much more civil to him than she was to you.'

Adam shrugged indifferently. 'Poor guy!' he said. 'But you and the old fella, I really thought you were a match.'

Eve bridled when he referred to Bill like that but she merely murmured, 'Sorry, but you are wrong.'

'Then why stay?' Alex demanded.

'I can't just walk out. I came especially to meet Bill. He is the only person I know in Australia.'

'Rubbish! You know lots of people: Chloe as well as Bill, the Malones, Adam, and now Fiona and me.' Eve had the feeling that Alex just stopped short of calling her a 'whingeing Pom'.

'Yes, but . . . '

'You don't have to stay with the McMahons if things are not working out — any more than I did,' Adam pointed out. 'Where is your spirit of adventure?'

Eve wanted to point out that it had been pretty adventurous to come to Australia in the first place but he went on, 'You should grab chances.'

Had Eve been looking at him instead of down into her tumbler she might have caught the gleam of mischief in his eyes and realized she was being sent up. 'What chances?'

'W-e-l-l . . . think how different it would have been if you had snatched me with one hand and opportunity with the other . . . ' He was grinning openly now.

Eve was tempted to throw her lemon drink at him.

'Have I missed something?' Alex looked from one to the other with a sardonic smile.

'No,' Eve snapped.

Adam mouthed 'Tell you later,' at Alex, who shrugged then glanced at his watch. Eve drained her glass and stood up.

'I am not trying to move you, Eve,' Alex apologized, 'but I have to go and see Fern in a few minutes.' He threw her a considering glance. 'Care to come with me?'

'Fern Barclay, the designer, who did this house? Oh, I'd love to, but I couldn't. I mean, she is not expecting me.'

Adam muttered, 'You see, you turn down opportunities.'

Eve tried hard to ignore him but could not miss the flicker of something that passed between the two men.

'I have to look after her cat,' Alex explained. 'She couldn't find anyone to stay in the house so she roped me in, her last desperate hope, got me at a weak moment. Cats are not my favourite people. Dogs, even that wretched little poodle of Fiona's, I can take, but cats scare me. They look right into you with those damn eyes of theirs and con you into believing they see into your very soul.'

'Maybe they just want to hypnotize you,' Adam suggested.

Eve smiled to herself. 'Is it a very special cat?' she asked. Fern probably chose her cat to match the décor.

Alex snorted with derision. 'Boss is an old moggy that belonged to the previous owner and refused to move out when she bought the cottage. Paul dubbed it Boss because that is just what it is — of her, anyway. Fern cajoled me into promising to go twice a day and feed the wretched creature. This afternoon I get my instructions.'

'Just what you wanted, to go inside her cottage.' Adam remembered Eve had said how she would love to see the interior. His eyes challenged her to grab the opportunity.

'You have to go back through Elmore anyway so it won't be out of your way.' Alex pointed out.

'I would like to come,' she told Alex, 'if you are sure Fern won't mind?'

'Absolutely. She loves people admiring her work. Are you coming too, Adam?'

'Wouldn't that really be an imposition?'

''Course not — the more the merrier. Travel with Eve and make sure she gets there, then you can come back with me.'

'I feel a sort of fellow feeling with you,' Adam surprised her by saying as she followed Alex's car away from the house.

'Oh — how come?'

'We are the guests who went wrong.'

11

'Is that why you gave me your mobile number?' Eve asked. 'Not that I expect to need it; I don't feel I have 'gone wrong'.'

'I'm sorry . . . ' He sounded totally unrepentant. 'But I didn't think things were going as planned with you and Bill . . . Another contact might be useful.'

'Well, you are wrong,' Eve lied, wishing he was. 'You are judging by your own experience; it is an easy thing to do.'

'That's because we are our own yardsticks.'

'Yes . . . ' Eve, not entirely sure what he meant, reverted to their earlier conversation. 'This may be the only chance I ever get to see the inside of Fern Barclay's own home, and I am taking it.'

'Good for you!' Adam approved as Eve pulled the car up behind Alex's rather flashy vehicle. At the front door they were greeted by a remarkably plain cat. He must, Eve thought, have hidden inner qualities for Fern to be so concerned for his welfare when she was away.

Alex put his finger on the bell and a few seconds later Fern's husband was ushering them inside. 'Fern is just finishing her packing,' he explained. 'I'm Paul and you . . . ?'

He looked from Eve to Adam and then to Alex, who quickly supplied, 'Adam and Eve,' with a quirky grin that challenged Paul to dispute this.

Paul's eyebrows shot up in a manner that succeeded in conveying polite amusement and disbelief. 'Adam and Eve — really?'

'Yes, really,' Adam cut in. 'We didn't know of each other's existence till we met . . . ' Eve held her breath, suddenly convinced he was going to say in bed. He paused just long enough to worry her before, with a mischievous smile, he added, 'Till we met at the McMahons for Christmas.'

As Fern burst into the room, the late afternoon sun slanting through the window caught her auburn hair so that it flamed in an aureole round her face. It gave her a vibrant, youthful attraction but Eve knew she was not far off her own age.

Introductions were repeated and her smile widened. 'Are you truly Adam and Eve or are you having me on?'

'It's true — scout's honour,' Alex said solemnly. 'They met when they were both house guests of the McMahons. When I mentioned to Eve that I had to come here to get my orders about Boss she jumped at the chance to see the inside of your house — she has admired what you did for Fiona and also read some of your articles.'

Eve glared and murmured, 'Alex suggested I come alon . . . ' but her words were lost as he continued, 'Eve greatly admired Boss when she saw him outside — she adores cats.' Not strictly accurate, but Fern's warm smile included both Eve and the cat, who was now ensconced in his favourite chair. He stared unblinkingly at Eve and she had the uncomfortable feeling that he knew exactly what she had thought about him. She turned back to Fern.

'I have to be sure he will be cared for when I have to go away,' she was explaining. 'You see, he was here before I was; sometimes I feel I live here courtesy of him rather than the other way round.'

'You bought him with the house?'

'Well sort of — except that I didn't know he was here when I bought the cottage. The agent didn't tell me.' Fern smiled at Paul, as if they shared some secret joke, and sensing the rapport between them Eve realized she had never known this sort of closeness with anyone.

'Those tins up there are for emergencies.' Fern had opened a cupboard door and was pointing out tins of cat food on one of the shelves to Alex. 'And I do mean emergencies — like when you absolutely run out of food. He much prefers fresh meat, liver, or heart, and he likes rabbit.' Every day would be an emergency, Alex decided. He was damned if he was going to spend his time shopping for gourmet cat food.

His thoughts were interrupted by Eve murmuring, with a touch of envy, 'I just love what you have done with this place — it must be marvellous to live here.'

Her words brought to the fore a vague idea that he knew had been hovering in the background for a while. He tuned back into the conversation to wait for the right moment to broach it.

'You should have seen it when she bought it,' Paul was saying to Eve. 'I couldn't believe she wanted it; I thought I would never sell it.'

'Did you own it then?' Eve was puzzled.

'Heavens, no! It was an estate sale — the poor old guy who owned it and had lived here for years died and the executors put it up for sale. Boss was the old man's cat; when he died no one thought about him so he went on living here as best he could.'

'Paul was working in real estate then,' Fern said by way of explanation.

'I see,' Eve said, although she didn't quite. 'He has gone back to his true calling now

— he is a head shrinker like me,' Alex put in.

'I see,' Eve once more murmured politely, wondering why Alex had that odd expression on his face.

'Why don't you then?' With a shock, Eve realized his question was directed at her. Had she missed something in the conversation?

'Why don't I what?'

'You just said you would love to live here,' Adam reminded her.

'I said it must be marvellous to live here.' Eve tried to remember exactly what she had said.

'Eve and Boss.' Eve had absently dropped her hand to the cat's head and he in turn was rubbing against it, purring. 'See!' Alex was jubilant.

'But — but — I can't . . . ' Eve stammered, then looking across at Adam, he gave her the thumbs-up sign, and she knew she could. But would Fern agree?

For a moment the only sound was rhythmic purring. Then everyone was talking at once and Eve discovered she had agreed to cat-sit for Fern for the next two weeks.

Now it was Eve who must be instructed in how to care for Boss and be teed up on the various things a person living in the house needed to know. 'You will find you can get just about all your day-to-day needs here in

Elmore and if you want to go further afield then I'm quite happy for you to use my car,' Fern explained.

'Oh, I couldn't do that!' Eve demurred.

'Why ever not? You do drive and have a licence, I suppose? It will only be standing in the carport otherwise as we are taking Paul's car.'

'Yes, but — Well, it just seems too much, a rent-free house and a car for my own use.'

'That is rubbish. You are the one doing me a favour.' She lowered her voice. 'Leaving Boss in Alex's care was a last desperate option. If Fiona had been home it would have been different but he doesn't like cats.' She looked anxiously at Eve. 'You like them, don't you? I know Boss is a plain old thing, but he came into my life when I was at a low ebb. So was he, and we each firmly believed the house was our very own. I guess he still does!'

Eve smiled; the more she knew of Fern the more she liked her.

'We are off in the morning. Will you be able to come sometime tomorrow?'

Eve still felt dazed as she climbed into Chloe's car to drive back. 'Goodbye, Alex — and thanks!'

'Thank *you*!' Alex retorted. 'You have taken over a chore I didn't want.'

'Goodbye, Adam. I don't suppose I shall see you again.'

'You probably will . . . I'm staying a few days with Alex, so I will say *au revoir*.'

Driving back, Eve realized that the one thing she had not done was have an in-depth conversation with Alex about his book and his strange ideas. The sun was in her eyes as she walked slowly up to the house with Chloe's car keys in her hand, and she didn't notice Bill sitting perfectly still in the deep old chair outside the house.

'So you are back.'

His voice startled her and she replied sharply, 'Didn't you think I would be?'

Bill shrugged. 'You could have still been there in a hypnotic trance.'

His voice was expressionless and Eve, unaware that he was teasing, flared back, 'I didn't get hypnotized — Alex didn't even suggest it.'

'That's too bad; you must be disappointed. Anyway, it's nice to see you home. I've been thinking about what we might do tomorrow . . . '

Eve stared at him, realizing that this was some sort of a peace offering to make up for his grumpiness earlier. Now her elation had evaporated and she felt bad about her promise to Fern. She wanted to accept Bill's olive branch, even extend one of her own. But she could not and she had to explain why.

12

Taking a deep breath, Eve explained, 'I — I don't think I will be here tomorrow.' Bill stared at her in frank disbelief. 'I'm sorry . . . ' she began.

'What do you mean? Of course you will be here tomorrow — where else would you be?' he interrupted.

'In Fern Barclay's cottage. I promised to look after her cat for her. Alex was going to feed it every day then he — '

'Hypnotized you into doing it for him,' Bill supplied, his voice scathing. 'Why on earth would you want to go and bury yourself up there in that old cottage all by yourself when you have a perfectly good place to stay here?' He paused, frowning slightly. 'You haven't taken umbrage over anything I said, have you?'

'Why should you think that?' The coolness of her tone masked the swift burning anger inside. 'You had every right to express your feelings but I was surprised that you should be so . . . ' She bit off the word rude. 'So . . . outspoken to someone who is a guest in your house.' Trying to be polite made her pompous.

Bill thought so too. 'Hoighty-toighty! I'm sorry if I touched a raw nerve; put it down to disappointment.' If he had stopped there all might have been well but he couldn't resist adding; 'You are, after all, a whingeing Pom.'

The last two words worked like a bellows on Eve's simmering anger. 'If I am a whingeing Pom then you are nothing better than a crude, rude Irish Aussie!' Try as she would, Eve could not keep her voice low. 'As for disappointment — well, that can be a two-way thing. God knows what you expected when you invited me out here to visit with you for Christmas.' Eve stopped short, her anger dying as swiftly as it flared, appalled at the implication of her words. She could feel the heat of embarrassment spreading from her throat to her cheeks and knew she had courted his angry response.

'I can assure you I didn't do this on purpose.' He gestured to his plastered ankle. 'If I had realized you expected someone more like that city ponce that Chloe invited instead of an old man with white hair and a broken ankle, I would have cancelled, not postponed your visit.'

'Stop feeling sorry for yourself. Your hair isn't white, it's going grey; neither are you old. As for that ankle — I am sure if you had wanted to you could . . . ' She stopped, appalled. What on earth had she been about to say? 'Oh, damn you!' she spluttered. Choking back angry tears, she turned away, almost colliding with Chloe. 'Sorry!' she gasped and thrust the car keys at her. 'Thank you — very much!' she managed, without pausing on her way to her room.

Chloe winced slightly as the bedroom door closed just short of a slam.

'What on earth is the matter with you two?' she demanded of her father. 'I heard you both yelling from the other side of the house! Quarrelling with a house guest doesn't make for a comfortable atmosphere.' Thinking of Adam, she had the grace to look sheepish.

'The pot calling the kettle black!' Bill was quick to remind her, adding in a sour tone, 'She is leaving in the morning.' Eve had not told him when she intended to leave but he didn't imagine, for either of their sakes, she would stay longer than necessary after their exchange.

'Leaving?' Chloe was astounded. 'I hoped . . .'

'Hope no more!' Bill snapped. 'And who are you to express an opinion about my affairs when you make such a mess of your own?' He struggled to his feet and with his crutches banging out an angry tattoo on the floor, headed indoors. 'If anyone wants me urgently I am working on my paperwork, with the 'Do Not Disturb' sign on the door.'

'But . . . ' Chloe was about to protest they didn't possess such a sign but of course he was talking in a symbolic not literal sense. She had been amazed to hear the yelling and was annoyed now with her father for, as she thought, driving Eve away just when she was beginning to like her. She had also been hurt when he turned his fury on her, totally unjustly. Her life was not in a mess; she had straightened it up when she sent Adam on his way. The realization that anything they had in common had vaporized when he arrived here had convinced her of the futility of trying to maintain a relationship. She shut off the thought that in her own environment she was not the same person as the one who had met Adam at a Sydney party.

Eve flung clothes into her suitcase, only to fling them out again when she discovered that she had no hope of closing the lid unless she made a better job of folding and packing. She wished she could walk out now, while her anger bubbled, but as Fern was not leaving till the next day it was hardly feasible.

Now she had calmed down, Eve was ashamed of herself. How could she have lost the plot and said those awful things? Now there was not only the rest of her time to get through but she must ask Chloe if she could drive her over to Fern's cottage in the morning.

A tap on her door made her heart race. 'Come in,' she called, and tried not to look downcast when she saw it was Chloe.

'Hi!' Chloe stared at Eve's packed case. 'You really are going?' Eve nodded. 'I'm sorry I interrupted you and Dad . . . ' She shrugged. 'But you *were* making a din.'

'I am the one who should apologize. I'm afraid I lost my temper and was probably very rude,' Eve admitted.

'You weren't the only one. You must have got his Irish dander up. I'm not blaming you,' she said hastily when Eve would have interrupted. 'He has been a bit touchy with that broken ankle of his — he is so mad he couldn't take you around . . . ' Chloe trailed off lamely. 'Look, what I really came in to say was, don't take Dad too seriously and please don't go because he has upset you.'

'It was because I told him I was leaving that day we had a row,' she explained, then rushed on with the rest of her story. 'I arrived at Alex's place just as he was off to see Fern Barclay because she hadn't found anyone to stay in her cottage and look after her cat while she was away and he had, reluctantly, agreed to go twice a day and feed it. He asked me to go with him; said it would be a wonderful chance to see the inside of her house. I don't quite know who suggested it or how it happened but I agreed to stay there. She very generously told me I can use her car while I am there but I have to get there . . . ' Eve's voice trailed off and she looked expectantly at Chloe, hoping she had guessed what she was about to ask.

'Good for you, getting to stay in that lovely cottage and use her car. I suppose the cat is something very exotic?'

'No, it is about the plainest old moggy I have ever met. She thinks the world of it though. She told me it lived there before she did.' Eve hesitated. The important question about how she was to get to Elmore in the morning seemed to have been lost in the discussion of the cat. 'What I wanted to ask you — do you think . . . ?'

'You won't have the car till you get there and you need transport — right?'

Eve was grateful to Chloe for grasping her need before she spelled it out. 'I feel bad asking you after . . . ' She was loath to bring up the subject of Bill.

'Try and stop me — I am just dying to see if the inside of the cottage is as nice as Fiona says.'

'Paul said it was a total wreck when she bought it.'

'He should know — he was the agent who sold it to her. That was how they met; Fiona told me they had both been married before.'

'They are a good couple — together, I mean.' Eve sounded wistful. She had come to Australia with warm and fuzzy notions about the outcome and now it had all blown sky-high.

Chloe thought it must be rough to be in a strange country and fight with the only people you knew. She had grown to like Eve very much and regretted the poor welcome she had given her. 'I could do with some help with that darn old cow if you have finished packing.' Her voice was gruff.

They got through the evening chores in record time. As they chopped and sliced in a companionable way for the evening meal, Eve almost regretted her impending departure now they had become good friends.

★　★　★

Eve was carrying her bag out to Chloe's car after breakfast when she heard the sound of Bill's crutches on the veranda. She could feel his eyes boring into her back and could not resist the urge to turn. Automatically she put her hand out to meet his held out in farewell. The tingle, almost amounting to a zap, as his fingers closed over hers, brought her eyes to his face. When he bent his head she raised her cheek for a farewell kiss, glad that they were not parting as enemies. Her breath came in a sharp intake when he gripped her hand tighter and kissed her full on her lips. Acting on its own volition, her body moved closer and she kissed him back with a depth and passion she had thought she'd left behind many years ago. It was a good feeling, till the angry words they had both spoken came between them and she pulled back.

'Goodbye, Bill, and thank you. I have enjoyed my slice of Australian rural life.' She pulled her hand free and turned quickly away before he could see the tears pricking behind her lids.

'Goodbye, Eve.' His voice was as stiff and formal as her own. 'Keep in touch.' Handling his crutches quite adroitly, Eve noticed, he turned away.

She watched him with a lump in her throat and didn't bother to go back in and check she had left anything behind.

Chloe tossed a book in her lap as she got in beside her.

'Take that with you — I see your bookmark is still in the middle. Keep it — I have read all I want to. It made me think, That poor guy needs to see a good psychologist!'

'But isn't he . . . ?' asked Eve, before catching on that Chloe was joking. 'Thank you very much. I would like to finish it, but don't you want it back?'

'Nope!' Chloe stated firmly as she lifted her foot from the brake and with a wave at the house moved forward. Eve turned and saw Bill leaning on his crutches in the doorway. She wished her visit was ending on a better note, even that she was not leaving at all, but the car was already out of the gate.

★ ★ ★

'Hi! You are here in good time.' Paul straightened up from the boot of the car. Eve wasn't sure whether he was pleased or not to see them so early. Then Fern flew out of the house, obviously ready to leave, with jacket and bag slung over her arm. She beamed.

'Great — you are here. I couldn't quite believe my luck yesterday. I feel much happier leaving Boss, and the cottage, of course, in your hands.' She thrust a business card at Eve. 'That has my mobile phone number on it, if you need me; hopefully I'll be in range.' Eve promised to contact her if need be, sure that Fern had left such good instructions that she would not have to, and watched her slip gracefully into the passenger seat beside Paul,

187

who already had the engine running.

'Do you suppose that copper-coloured hair is natural?' Chloe mused as she turned to help Eve get her bags from the car.

'I hadn't thought about it.' Eve lied, aware of sounding elderly and prim. 'Come on, let's see if we can rustle up a cup of coffee.'

Boss, on the most comfortable chair, treated them to a cool and, Eve thought, rather disdainful stare. Chloe stared back. 'Fern's taste in décor certainly doesn't extend to cats,' was her dry comment. 'I would have expected her to have a Siamese at least.'

'I told you — she didn't choose him. He sort of came with the house from what I can gather,' Eve reminded Chloe as she switched on the electric jug and looked for mugs. Fern had shown her where the coffee was and had promised to leave milk and such basics in the fridge for her. Chloe looked round her with frank curiosity and followed Eve to the bedroom, where she took her case.

'It is nice,' she conceded, 'but I should have expected her to have something, well, a bit grander than this.'

'Maybe grandeur is not her thing, and anyway I gather she has an apartment or something, maybe even a house, in Melbourne. Sounds as if the jug is boiling.' Eve led the way back to the kitchen feeling vaguely resentful of any hint of criticism of Fern, her house, and even her cat. She was eager to speed Chloe on her way so that she could enjoy being alone in this enchanting cottage, which she could already feel enfolding her in its own special ambience.

13

'Don't you think you will be lonely here?' Chloe asked as she sipped her coffee.

'I don't mind being on my own,' Eve assured her, then wondered if maybe that was somewhat tactless so hastily added, 'I shall miss you — and your father, I expect. But as I have Fern's car I can explore the neighbourhood, even come over and see you, if you will have me.'

'Of course we will — I expect by now Dad is feeling pretty bad about you coming here. After all, you were his guest — he was the one who asked you to stay with us in the first place.'

'Not entirely. I mean, it was more or less a case of me inviting myself as much as him asking me,' Eve admitted. 'I had some money to spare for about the first time in my life and Australia had always interested me — more than that, fascinated me. It was one place I really wanted to see before I died, which was why I had a penfriend, if that is what you call Internet friends, here in the first place. Your dad and I got on really well. I thought — ' She stopped abruptly before she said something she might regret. 'I thought Christmas in the sun would be a change, which it certainly has been. I have enjoyed myself but nothing lasts for ever, as they say. I didn't want to outstay my welcome . . . ' Eve knew she was beginning to gabble and was afraid she might also sound vague and twittery. She shrugged. 'I'm grateful to you, Chloe, both of you.'

'I have enjoyed having you,' Chloe admitted. 'I am really sorry things didn't work out with you and Dad.' She grinned. 'If nothing else it would have let me off the hook.'

'Meaning?'

'Well, if you had decided to stay and make a life here with Dad, I would not have had to worry about him — I could have gone off and lived my own life with perfect freedom.'

'Is that what you really want to do, Chloe?'

'Yes — yes, it is. Hell, no — not entirely. The truth is I miss the bush, the farm, the animals, my friends here.'

'You can take the girl out of the country but you can't take the country out of the girl. That's about the size of it, so why not stay?'

'No, I can't. When I came back for Christmas I thought — I hoped — No, I couldn't stay now.' Chloe knew she couldn't bear the thought of seeing Gary and Maureen together.

Eve wondered how anyone could be as blind as Chloe, not only it seemed about the way Steve felt for her but, she suspected, her own feelings for Steve. 'Your father would like you to stay. So would Steve.'

'Whatever makes you think that? Steve is my surrogate brother; he sees me as just another sister. But Dad — yes, he would like me to stay.'

'I got the impression Steve would too,' Eve persisted.

Chloe gazed thoughtfully into her empty coffee cup then, as if she had found inspiration in it, pushed it away and jumped to her feet, rattling her car keys. 'I must go. If you get lonely, just sing out.'

Eve sat on at the kitchen bench after she left, cradling another cup of coffee and fighting the sudden conviction that she had done something very stupid. The slamming of a car door brought her back to the moment and she walked over to the window. She thought Adam had a sensuous walk; he reminded her of a panther or a leopard.

'You just missed Chloe.' Wondering why he had come, she said the first thing that came into her head.

'Good,' he said succinctly. 'Alex sent me to see if you had arrived, if you were settling in all right, if there was anything you wanted, and of course to make sure you are discharging your duties as far as the cat is concerned.'

So he was here because Alex sent him. 'Everything is just fine. Come in and see for yourself.'

'Well, at least I can assure Alex that he hasn't left home yet.' He crossed the room to the sleeping cat and touched him lightly between the ears. Boss stirred with a small 'Prrt' of greeting and rubbed his head on his hand.

'He likes you.' She should have spoken to the cat herself; Adam was joking but how would she ever explain to Fern if Boss did walk out?

'I like cats — far more than I do cows,' Adam admitted.

'I can see that.' Eve couldn't repress a smile at the memory of Adam after his disastrous encounter with a cow. 'How long are you staying with Alex?'

'That depends.' His answer was so long in coming that she wondered if he had heard. 'Mainly on how long I can manage without blotting my copybook.'

'Neither of us started off well at the McMahons'.' Eve immediately wished she had not brought up that wretched incident.

'We labelled ourselves 'undesirable guests'

before we had been there twenty-four hours,' Adam agreed. 'Then you and the old guy seemed to be getting along well enough, so why did you leave?'

Eve began to protest that Bill was not old, but did it really matter what Adam thought? She certainly had no intention of launching into explanations. 'We just — Well, we didn't have much in common,' she said lamely. 'What about you and Chloe?' Two could ask questions.

'Just a stupid thing that should never have happened. I can't believe the silly girl can't see that Steve has eyes for no one but her — except that horse of his, of course.' His grin had a wry twist to it at the reference to Golden Dollar.

'Yeah,' Eve drawled thoughtfully, 'everybody else it seems is very well aware about how Steve feels about her except Chloe.' She sighed, wondering what — if anything — could be done. 'I suppose one can't arrange other people's love lives for them,' she finally acceded. Especially, she thought, if one can't fix one's own.

Adam moved to the door. 'I can report to Alex that both you and the cat are alive and well.' He looked down at her, one hand on the latch. Eve was taken by surprise when he put his hands on her shoulders. 'We can't organize other people's lives, but at least we can try to do something about our own.' Then he bent and kissed her swiftly on the lips before turning and striding away down the path.

Eve stared after him. 'Come again any time . . .' she stammered, but by the time the words were uttered he was closing the garden gate behind him and getting in his car. He raised one hand to her as he slid into the driving seat.

A review of the contents of the fridge and small walk-in pantry revealed a more than adequate stock of cat food and little else. Gathering money and shopping bags, she set off to explore and forage.

★　★　★

Chloe was turning the corner when she saw a car stop at the house she had just left. Who would be visiting Eve so soon after her arrival? She kept her eye on the rear-vision mirror and thought she must be hallucinating when she saw Adam turn in at the garden gate. Her first impulse was to turn round and confront the two of them, but fear of looking a complete fool stopped her. It was, after all, no business of hers what either of them did. All the same, she tingled with curiosity.

Maybe she had been correct to accuse Eve of being after every man she met? She felt disillusioned, not with Adam but with Eve, whom she had grown to really like, even to the point of regretting that things hadn't worked out.

At home Chloe found Steve sitting on the veranda drinking beer with her father. She put Adam out of her mind. 'That looks good — I'll get one and join you.' As she climbed the steps, both men abruptly stopped their conversation. 'Yeah — do,' her father said. Steve just smiled.

'You don't have to stop talking just because I am here,' Chloe protested.

'We were only farming.'

'Then go on farming, Dad. My presence has never stopped you before.' She intercepted the guilty look that flashed between the two men.

'I hear you have lost your house guest,' Steve remarked, too casually, after a prolonged pause. 'Is she coming back?'

Into the uncomfortable silence that followed, Chloe dropped another clanger: 'Adam arrived at the house just as I was leaving.'

'You mean Fern's place?' There was a sharp edge to Bill's voice. 'Is he staying there too?'

'I don't know, Dad.' The possibility hadn't

crossed her mind till this moment but now the idea had been presented to her she thought it was a probability rather than a possibility. 'If he is then you and I have both been stood up. Maybe they have been planning this.' Even though part of her said she was taking a dog-in-the-manger attitude, she felt both hurt and angry and turned furiously on Steve when he gave a snort of laughter. 'Is that so funny?'

'Be reasonable, Chloe, I am sure Eve is not the type to rush off to sleep with another man when she had come here expressly to meet your father. Or did you surprise them in bed together?'

'I saw him drive up to Fern's gate as I was driving away.'

'Don't you think there could have been any number of quite innocent explanations for that?'

'Well, it wouldn't be the first time.' Too late, she remembered that as far as she knew, neither man knew the story of Eve and Adam's unconventional meeting.

Bill wished Chloe had not reminded him of that. When Eve told the story it had sounded amusing and quite innocent; now he had doubts. He recalled Eve explaining about Fern offering her the cottage. 'I don't want to talk about it. They have both gone and they are free agents. But Steve is right — it is silly to assume things when there could be a good explanation.'

Steve, his eyes on Chloe, swallowed the last of his beer. 'Come on, drink up,' he told her, 'then go put your boots on and come back with me. Riding Crispin will clear your head and I need some help moving some stock.'

Chloe glowered at him, but did as he suggested and finished her beer before going inside to change into an old pair of jeans and collect her hat and boots.

★ ★ ★

Steve watched her making a quick mental inventory of his cattle and deciding which ones to move. All he knew about Adam was that he was no longer around, which left him free to make the most of his time with Chloe before school started again.

Chloe had been correct, they had not been discussing farming when she arrived home. Bill, disappointed himself in his failure to make any headway with Eve, had pointed out that it was time for Steve to make it clear to Chloe that his feelings for her were not those of a brother. 'You have a clear run now that fellow she brought with her has gone and if you don't take advantage of it she will be off again herself.' If what Chloe had said was true, then Adam had not gone far.

He was planning his next move when Chloe came back, riding boots on her feet and hat in hand. In her other hand she had a slip of paper which she shook at him to emphasize her words.

'I found this in Eve's room when I went in to get the old boots I had lent her.' She thrust the paper at her father. 'This is Adam's writing and Adam's mobile phone number. I recognize them both.'

Bill took the paper reluctantly; even before he read it he knew it spelt the end of his hopes and dreams.

14

Eve made sure Boss was inside when she left the cottage, and set off for the main shopping street. By the time she got back she was regretting the bag of apples she had bought and the large bottle of orange juice but changed her mind when she savoured both in the tranquillity of the garden. As she peeled an apple, she wondered what Adam was really doing here in Elmore. Did he hope to meet up with Chloe again or was Alex's explanation the truth? Would she, she wondered, see him again or was he already on his way to wherever it was he was going?

She opened Alex's book, which she had brought out with her. She thought it read more like fiction than a serious textbook on psychology; she could not take it seriously but Alex wrote in a way that made you continue.

When she was shopping people had commented on the pleasant coolness of the day but to Eve it was hot and her lids grew heavy. She adjusted the garden lounge so that she was almost horizontal and kicked off her sandals. She was vaguely aware that her eyes had closed and felt the book drop but when a voice close by penetrated her senses she forced her lids up and groped for the book as she struggled to collect her wits.

'I knocked loud and long on the front door before I came round here to the back,' Alex told her as he handed her the book with a wry look at the cover. 'Nice to know you find this so riveting.'

'Oh — but I did — I think you have a very readable way of writing.'

He smiled wryly at the palpable lie and pulled up a garden chair for himself.

Eve pulled herself to a sitting position and complained, 'You might as well have looked after the cat yourself,' she told him, 'if you are going to come round morning and night to check on me.'

'I didn't come this morning.'

'Well, you sent Adam — same difference,' she retorted peevishly.

'You haven't told me what you think of my book.'

'I don't think you want to know.'

'Oh, but I do — I like hearing all viewpoints.'

Eve didn't really believe him but she began, 'I think it is a . . . ' She had been about to say 'a load of old rubbish' but muttered instead, 'I don't agree with any of it.'

'Not any of it?'

201

'Not any of it,' she repeated remorselessly. 'Reincarnation is a terrifying prospect. It is just about impossible to get one life right; coming back to do it all over again is a horrendous thought. As for dreams, they are just the result of an overactive mind winding down during sleep, or too much rich food before bed.'

'You have studied psychology?' The question was bland but there was an edge to his voice.

'I can still have an opinion.' Eve was defensive.

'Of course. Everyone is entitled to an opinion.' His tone of voice told Eve that one that was at odds with his was negligible.

'Do you believe in ghosts?' The question, breaking the silence between them, took her by surprise.

'Of course not,' she snapped without bothering to give it much thought.

'Fern was bothered by very odd dreams; she thought the house had a resident spirit. You don't strike me as being the imaginative type.'

Eve did not feel he intended this as a compliment and snarled back, 'I suppose that is a fancy way of telling me the damn house is haunted.'

Alex merely shrugged. After a few moments'

silence he pushed himself to his feet and held out his hand to her. 'I'll say goodbye. I do hope I haven't disturbed you. You and the cat both seem fine.'

Unable to think of a reply of any sort, Eve mumbled some sort of 'Goodbye' and retrieved her hand.

As day gave way to evening and then night, Eve felt her enchantment with the cottage wearing thin; Alex's mocking words had honed in on a weak spot in her psyche. She reiterated to herself that she had no time for his nonsensical ideas and did her best to lift the atmosphere in the house but the gloomy news on radio and TV were little help, so she raided Fern's CD tower and brightened as Fiona's voice rippling through the house lifted her spirits. When she went to bed she left a table lamp alight in the living room and another in the bedroom. With the bedside radio set to the classical music station, she plumped up the pillows and settled down to finish Alex's book. Determined to be sensible, she switched off both the radio and the light and fell instantly asleep.

She woke with Alex's words playing in her head, and knew that on one point at least he had been wrong. Her imagination was firing on all cylinders. If it wasn't then someone was sitting on the end of her bed, almost on her feet. With extreme caution she moved one and encountered something. She froze and lay still, the beating of her own heart thudding in her ears. There was no other sound so, very gingerly, she fumbled for the switch on the bedside lamp.

The human figure she half-expected was not on the end of her bed. She raised herself slowly on her elbows. When she saw the cat curled up against her feet, fast asleep, she didn't know whether to laugh and let him stay or kick him off. Her sense of humour won; after all, this was his house and in all probability this was where he always slept. Besides, even a sleeping cat was better company than none. All the same, she left the light on as she pulled the sheet over her shoulders.

Next time she opened her eyes sun was filtering through the drapes and the cat had moved up the bed to sit on the pillow, staring at her. She guessed he had breakfast in mind.

As she jiggled a teabag and watched the hot water darken, Boss was already halfway through a large saucer of milk. She wondered how to fill the empty day ahead. A house all to herself and freedom to fill her days as she chose did not seem quite as appealing now it was a reality and two whole weeks stretched ahead.

Remembering the day in Daylesford with Bill, she was filled with nostalgia. How good it would be to have his company; the prospect of lonely sightseeing did not enthrall.

She continued to think about how to fill the day while she showered. Most of her best ideas had come to her over the years in the shower or the bath; it must be the relaxing effect of warm water, she thought.

This morning it didn't work. She emerged, dried herself and dressed, then sat down at the kitchen bench again to eat toast and honey and drink coffee. She was just finishing when the ringing phone jolted her out of her unproductive reverie.

She had not expected to hear from Alex and was only aware of faint irritation laced with disappointment as she recognized his voice. She waited for him to ask if she had seen the ghost but he said without preamble, 'Adam is leaving today.'

'Oh.' There seemed nothing else to say. 'I'm sorry' or 'I shall miss him' seemed over the top.

She tried to take in what Alex was saying. 'He is driving back to Sydney. We could go as far as Echuca and meet him for lunch.' When she didn't answer immediately he added, 'Unless you have already planned your day.'

In the short silence that followed, Eve's thoughts embraced all the pros and cons of his suggestion. 'Thank you,' she said at last, adding as something clicked in her memory,

'*All the Rivers Run?* That is set in Echuca, isn't it? It's years since I read it.' She looked thoughtful for a moment. 'I think I saw a copy in Fern's bookcase.' Other people's bookcases gave so much away about them.

She looked down at her clothes, jeans, albeit good ones, and a decent shirt — suitable wear for a tourist — improved her make-up, combed her hair, collected her bag and the ubiquitous hat and sunglasses then, with a last look in the mirror, decided she would do. A glance at her watch told her she still had ten to fifteen minutes in hand — Alex had given her thirty minutes. She pulled Nancy Cato's novel out of the bookcase. The blurb told her it was a great love story set in Echuca in the 1890s — telling her what she was looking for, the period in which it was set.

Remembering Boss had gone outside after his morning milk, she returned the book to its place and hurried to call him in. She was far too conscious of her responsibility as a cat-sitter to leave him out for the day.

★ ★ ★

'For you,' Alex told her, handing her a packet from the passenger seat. 'Well, temporarily — on loan, that is.'

Eve found a DVD of the TV series of *All the Rivers Run*. 'Oh!' she exclaimed in delight. 'Thank you. I will enjoy this.'

'If you haven't had enough of Echuca by tonight. I am probably doing this in the wrong order — you should watch those *before* I take you up to Echuca.'

'I thought Adam was coming with us.' Eve glanced over her shoulder, as if suspecting that he might be hidden in the back seat somewhere.

'In his own car. We will meet him in Echuca.'

'Ah, yes, of course.' Realizing she had asked a stupid question, Eve decided to relax and enjoy the journey and not try and make intelligent conversation.

All roads in Echuca appeared to lead to the 'Mighty Murray'. Eve was enchanted by the paddle steamers. 'Until I read *All the Rivers Run* I thought paddle steamers were unique to America and the Mississippi.'

'What a good job you read it then.' Alex gave her a sidelong grin. 'We are meeting Adam at a restaurant in the centre of town for an early lunch so that he can get on his way in good time,' he told her as he turned the car away from the river.

★ ★ ★

Adam, sipping a glass of white wine, smiled and raised his glass as they joined him at the table.

'Not a bad drop,' he told them, picking up the bottle to fill their glasses. The choice of restaurant had been good: food, surroundings, service and wine were all excellent. Adam, at ease as she had never seen him, was in no hurry to be on his way and as the meal progressed Eve found she was really enjoying his company and understood how Chloe had come to invite him to stay for Christmas. Their mutual inability to be wholly successful as guests of the McMahons, together with their shared memories of their unconventional meeting, created a link between them. Eve was sorry when he made a move to continue his journey, and felt a frisson of irritation with Alex for encouraging him.

'Paddle steamers next, I think, assuming you still want to see them,' Alex said, when he'd gone.

They arrived at the wharf as passengers were loading for a short trip on the river. 'Come on.' Alex brooked no argument, and with his hand under her elbow he steered her on board. 'We might as well do things properly.'

Eve needed no urging; the sound of the water as the paddle turned fired her imagination and she could easily imagine herself back in the late nineteenth century.

15

Bill watched Chloe yank her boots on and ram her hat down on her head so firmly he almost winced himself. He could see she was either angry or upset about something. He watched her through half-closed eyes, sleep but a blink away. The sun was warm and the beer he had just consumed had induced in him a state of reflection. He was thinking about Eve, whom he had liked far more than he dared hope or expect, yet he had let her go. Worse, they had parted with a distinct coolness between them. While he was not prepared to admit that it had been entirely his fault, he had, perhaps, been too outspoken. But he couldn't for the life of him see why she would choose to spend time alone in a small place like Elmore when she was supposed to be his house guest. He might give her a ring and see how she was getting along. If it wasn't for this blasted ankle of his, he could drive up and see her, but he would phone her. He might even get around to apologizing, though he wasn't quite sure what for. Then he remembered the note Chloe had found; he put his hand in his pocket and felt it still there. How stupid to have kept it, but not as stupid as imagining there was any hope left for him as far as Eve was concerned.

Chloe, he thought, looked about as glum as he felt. Was she regretting letting Adam go? 'You know, Dad, that note could have meant anything — it may not even have been written to Eve.' Seeing her father so down in the dumps made her regret ever mentioning Adam. After all, there was the possibility that it had been someone else she had seen, and the note — well, she had just given a possible explanation for that.

'Of course it was for her,' Bill snapped. 'You brought it to my notice, so don't start making excuses for her. She has gone now and I intend to forget her.' He had now abandoned all stupid notions about calling Eve on the phone and certainly as far as apologizing — there was absolutely nothing on his side to apologize for. He struggled to his feet and glared at his daughter. 'You off helping Steve move their stock again?'

'No, he is helping me move ours.' She was equally abrupt.

Bill shrugged and, leaning heavily on his crutches, hobbled inside. 'I still have paper-work to struggle with. At least I have time to get it up to date now.'

'Thanks, Alex, that was a wonderful trip.' Eve smiled her thanks as she opened the car door. She tapped the DVD that he had lent her. 'And for this — I'll watch it tonight and maybe have another look at the book in bed tonight. Won't you come in for a drink?'

Alex shook his head. 'No, thanks all the same. It was a good day, wasn't it? But don't overdose on old Echuca — it might make you dream.' Eve acknowledged his smile with one of her own.

Eve slept deep and dreamlessly. She had once read that we always dream but do not remember, though she was sure that if she did not recall anything it was because she had not dreamed during the night. She was glad Boss settled on the bed before she dropped off to sleep; as he obviously considered it his place she didn't feel justified in stopping him but it had unnerved her when she thought someone was sitting on the end of her bed.

By evening the following day Eve was not so sure it had been a good idea to move into Fern's cottage. It was of course her own fault that she had not left it all day but neither had she seen anyone or spoken to another soul on the phone. To spend an entire day reading, watching DVDs or listening to CDs, all of which she could have done at home without the expense of a flight to Australia, struck her as absurd. She picked up the silent phone and pressed the call button. The dialling tone hummed in her ear but who did she expect to call? Adam was well on his way out of her life; it had been fun meeting up with him again but she did not hanker after his company. Alex had already given up one day to her, and the only other people she knew were Bill and Chloe. She held the phone in her hand. Should she call them?

Finally she went to bed, still without speaking to anyone but determined not to waste another day of her time in Australia. She could drive up to Rochester; it had struck her as being a pleasant little town when they drove through on their way to Echuca. She remembered the outing to Daylesford with Bill. They had succeeded in recapturing the easy friendship that had characterized their Internet chatting. Making a firm resolve to talk to him over the phone next day, put whatever it was that seemed to have gone wrong between them right and maybe spend more time there before she left Australia, she drifted off to sleep.

That night she did dream. She remembered standing at a closed door knocking; just when she was giving up hope it opened and she saw a man with swirls of either fog or smoke, she couldn't be sure which, almost hiding him. When it cleared she was staring at Bill but even as they recognized each other his eyes became blank and the door slammed. The rejection was so total and so unexpected that she still felt it as she opened her eyes reluctantly to a new day. She turned her head into the pillow with a stifled groan, surprised to note that the bedside clock told her that it was a good half hour-later than her usual wake-up time. She could still hear the knocking of her dream; she was fully awake before she realized the sound was coming from her own front door.

'Go away!' she muttered out loud, then changed it to, 'Oh, all right, I'm coming!' when whoever it was just went on knocking.

She stumbled out of bed, snatched up her robe and hurried to the door.

'You woke me up!' she accused. 'It is far too early to make a social call.'

'Do you realize the time?' Alex looked her up and down critically, making Eve wish she had left him on the doorstep while she dressed, or at least ran a comb through her hair. He confirmed this when he added, 'If I may say so, you look awful.'

'No, you may not say so. As a psychologist you must know comments like that are disastrous to the selfesteem of the recipient.'

'Especially when they are true.' He was quite unabashed. 'Can I come in or must I stay on the doorstep?'

'You can come in if you want to.' It was not a gracious invitation because truthfully she would have preferred him to stay where he was — or better still, go away.

'I'll make coffee while you dress.' Eve glared at him, simmering inwardly as he calmly took charge. 'And shower,' he called after her retreating back.

Determined not to hurry, she washed her hair as well. Reappearing clean, sweet-smelling and neatly dressed to coffee bubbling cheerfully in Fern's percolator, she could almost forgive Alex for what she had first considered his unwarranted intrusion. Toast popping up in the toaster added to her feeling of wellbeing.

But when Alex commented in an irritatingly motherly voice, 'That's more like it!', she responded with a frosty glare and a mumbled 'Thanks' before sitting down at the breakfast bar.

Alex poured coffee for them both then sat to watch her drink hers and spread honey on the toast. The sound of Eve chewing filled the silence till finally she was forced to demand, 'Why are you here so early?'

'To see you — why else? I don't call almost ten in the morning early.'

'Is there any more coffee?' Eve flinched at her own rudeness and reminded of her responsibility asked, 'Has what's-his-name, Boss, had milk?

'He would not be giving himself a thorough after-brekky wash if he had not.'

Eve cast a sour look at the cat ensconced as usual in the most comfortable chair and, as Alex had pointed out, washing himself with great concentration. 'It is empty!' she accused as her fingers closed round the milk carton.

'Yeah — I told you I'd fed him.'

With a resigned sigh, Eve drank her coffee black, casting a disgruntled look at both Alex and Boss. 'I'm not entirely sure I like this cottage, after all. It has . . . ' She broke off, reluctant to give Alex the satisfaction of saying 'I told you so'.

'A ghost?' He sounded hopeful.

'Of course not.' She almost added, 'But it does have an atmosphere'. But the very idea was anathema; it was as absurd to imagine that a house could have a special atmosphere of its own as it was to believe in ghosts.

'Tell me about your dream,' Alex startled her by asking.

'I don't dream — ever. What makes you think I did last night?'

'People who wake up as grumpy as you seem to be have usually dreamt in some disturbing fashion. You don't believe in ghosts, so . . . ' He shrugged.

'Very clever deduction. Perhaps you can tell me what I was dreaming about? Except,' she added, 'that I didn't dream.'

Alex stood up and moved to the door. 'Perhaps I should come back when your mood has improved.'

Eve, embarrassed by her own attitude, mumbled an apology. 'I'm sorry . . . I don't know what has got into me this morning. I — I'm not usually this . . . '

'Disagreeable,' Alex supplied.

'I was going to say rude,' she admitted. 'I'm sorry,' she repeated. 'I guess you caught me out. Sit down and have another coffee.'

He sat down again and reached for the coffee pot. 'It seems rather empty.' He gave it a small shake to prove his point.

Eve jumped up. 'I'll recharge it.'

Alex watched her in silence, only speaking when their cups were full once more. 'Well, are you going to unburden yourself of this dream of yours, or not?' Perhaps because he sounded as if he didn't really care either way, Eve was piqued into telling him.

16

'Is that all?' Alex sounded disappointed.

'It was quite enough for me. I suppose you hoped I met your 'spirit of the house' in my dreams.

'You had a short and simple dream no doubt evoked by your subconscious hearing me banging on your door and, of course, your own guilty conscience.'

'Why should I have a guilty conscience?'

Alex shrugged; something he did a mite too often, Eve thought sourly. 'You tell me. I'm off now I have checked on you both.'

'Both?'

'You and the cat, of course.'

'Of course.'

Eve found herself resisting a strong impulse to hurl something at the door as it closed behind him. Absurdly, she felt slighted by his lack of interest in her dream but told herself she was glad she was not interesting enough to merit a mention in his next book.

Snatching up her purse, she walked briskly to the nearest milk bar to replace the milk drunk by Boss. Alex may have dismissed her dream but it filled her thoughts as she walked. The feeling of total rejection as she watched Bill's expression go blank was still with her. Maybe she *should* call him but she was half-afraid of a real-life reaction similar to the dream one. The weather was so beautiful she took a roundabout route home. Looking forward to a decent cup of coffee she realized she was also hungry; breakfast may have been late but not very satisfying. She made herself a cheese and tomato sandwich and more coffee, added an apple to the tray and took it outside.

She tried to empty her mind and relax in the attractive surroundings but her thoughts turned relentlessly to Alex. Aware that she, who prided herself on her good manners, had been scarcely civil to him, she tried to compose some sort of apology in her head. Then dismissed the idea; she seemed to be worrying most of the time about how to put right things she had said. She would also forget that silly dream. She had come to Australia to enjoy herself, not agonize over trivialities. As for Bill McMahon, well, they would either continue their relationship in cyber space or more likely it would cease altogether. The likelihood of anything else was zilch. At least her trip to Australia had put an end to foolish dreams. But she missed them. Giving herself a mental shake, she jumped to her feet. What had happened to her planned trip to Rochester? The phone rang as she returned to the house.

'Alex . . . ?'

'Hi, Eve. You sound odd — nothing wrong, is there?'

'Good heavens, no — nothing at all. I had just been thinking about you, wondering if I should phone you. I sort of feel I owe you an apology.'

He laughed. 'If I had to say sorry to everyone I was a bit grumpy with I would never say anything else. But if you feel strongly about it, and have nothing better to do, why not join me in a cup of tea? But I should warn you, I've nothing but tea.'

'I'll call in at the baker and bring something.'

'Then I can expect you?'

'Well — yes.' Eve was annoyed with herself for agreeing to something she didn't particularly want to do. Urbane and charming though he could be, she found him unsettling. As a boost to her own confidence, she discarded her jeans and runners for skirt and sandals.

It was mid-afternoon and hot by the time she arrived and she was thinking wistfully of a siesta in the cool bedroom of the old cottage. Australia, with a climate so like Spain, should take the siesta to its heart.

Come into my parlour said the spider to the fly, she thought wildly as she switched off the engine and saw Alex framed in the open doorway. She wondered by what devious power he had persuaded her to come, and even bring food with her.

'Peace offering,' she murmured, holding out her purchase. She followed him into the lounge, where he placed a tray carefully on a small table between two armchairs. Eve wondered if he would ask her to be 'mother' and pour but he picked up the teapot himself. Watching him, Eve conceded that he was a very attractive man, then amended this in her mind to good-looking; he did not attract her one bit. At this moment her feeling was that of a schoolgirl summoned to the head's study. 'I really feel I should apologize for the way I was this morning,' she began.

'When you say you 'should' or you 'ought', that is a sure sign you don't want to do something,' Alex told her, 'so let's just take it as read, shall we? I should also apologize for disturbing you so early in the morning.' Eve said nothing, but gratefully sipped her tea. Alex looked at her over the rim of his own cup. 'But you were quite ... ' He shrugged, letting the unfinished sentence hang in the air.

'It was early — I — I didn't sleep too well. You woke me with a start . . . ' Her voice died as her catalogue of weak excuses came to an end. She put down her cup and took a chocolate chip cookie. 'These are quite good,' she told him through a mouthful of crumbs, wondering how soon obligatory good manners would allow her to escape. He was looking at her over the rim of his own cup in that unnerving way again, something he had not done once on their day out in Echuca. He had not been in what she termed to herself psychologist mode, at all then.

When the silence became uncomfortable, she asked how long Fiona expected to be away. 'Has she taken Beau with her?' she asked. There had been no sign or sound of the little poodle since she arrived.

'She has not. The wretched dog is sulking on her bed. She decided not to take him at the last minute.'

Eve thought it probable that the dog found Alex a poor substitute for his mistress. She was remembering his reluctance to care for Boss when he said, 'I'm glad you took on the job of looking after that spoilt cat,' making her wonder if he really could tune into her thoughts. 'But maybe it wasn't such a good thing for you.'

'A cottage and a car all for free for a couple

of weeks? What more could anyone want?'

'In a small place like Elmore — a good deal, I should have thought. You won't see much of the real Australia here.'

'But what exactly *is* the real Australia? I should have thought a small town like this was pretty representative, and it is very central, just about in the middle of Victoria, easy to get to Echuca, Bendigo, Shepparton, and I have discovered I can get by bus to Melbourne.'

'Victoria is *not* Australia — it is just one state. You should be seeing some of the others while you are here.'

Secretly Eve had been thinking along those lines herself, but when she looked at a map of Australia its very vastness had daunted her. 'One state at a time is enough for me. Anyway, I didn't come here on a 'see Australia' mission.'

'You came to see Bill McMahon. So why are you here in Elmore?'

'Can you ever stop being a psychologist?' Eve almost snarled.

'Probably not.' Alex was unruffled. 'When you have a passion for what you do it becomes part of you. Fiona could never not be a singer, in the same way Fern, I am sure, is always an interior designer. How about you?'

'I'm afraid I cannot think of anything that I am really passionate about. There are things I like, of course, but they are not really a part of me. I suppose I am just a very ordinary woman,' Eve admitted.

'No one is completely ordinary. There is something special about each one of us; the trick is finding it.'

'Then I guess I haven't.' Eve wondered if she could make a move to leave. She had no wish to become part of Alex's passion for analysing other people.

'Maybe goodness, as in virtue, doing the right thing, is your passion.'

'Alex, I am quite sure you are very clever, far too clever for me . . . ' Eve tried to keep her temper. What she really wanted to do was yell and protest that he didn't know a thing about her, and psychologist or not he had got her all wrong but, 'I can't see much passion in trying to do the right thing,' was all she said.

Alex ignored her. 'No doubt you were a good little girl who in due course became a good wife and a good mother. Didn't you find it dull?'

Eve was on the point of admitting that she had, sometimes, when he added, grinning, she thought malevolently, 'It is said that the good ones are always dull.'

It was only much later that Eve admitted to herself that she was so furious because she had a sneaking feeling that he was right.

She jumped to her feet, unconsciously smoothing the front of her skirt in an odd, and rather prim, gesture. 'I'm going.' She was not in the mood for niceties. 'I — I have things to do. Goodbye!' As she stormed out with as much dignity as she could muster, Eve had the uncomfortable feeling that behind her Alex was immensely amused — at her expense.

Alex Cameron, she decided, as she left in a spurt of dust, was the most arrogant and irritating person she had ever met, and if she never met him again it would be far too soon. When she hit the highway she kept on driving. She might as well fall back on her original plan and go to Rochester; it was still only mid-afternoon.

She had thought it a pleasant and typically Australian small town when they drove through it on their way to Echuca, although if asked what that was she would have found it hard to describe. She had come to expect wide straight streets, often running parallel to one another in a sort of grid pattern. She parked the car in the centre of the town and wandered round. It was a compact little town and by the time the shops began to close and the light showed signs of fading she felt she had seen most of it. She went to a fish and chip shop and bought her evening meal, with an extra piece of fish for Boss. Thinking of him in this way gave her a pleasant little glow of virtue, till she realized that Alex would certainly say she was running true to form, trying to please someone else — in this case the cat. She turned up the radio in the car; Alex had talked a lot of rubbish.

Later on, when she and Boss were enjoying their meal, she wondered if there might be a grain of truth in his words. Were good people invariably dull? Worse — was *she* dull? Was that why things (she didn't actually specify in her mind what she meant by things) had not really progressed between her and Bill? She thought of him as good, but she had not found him dull. Had he been bored with her? Maybe she should contact him. She had to admit Alex was right there: when you used 'should' to yourself it meant you didn't really want to do whatever it was. It wasn't that she didn't want to talk to Bill but that she was afraid he had written her off. All the same . . .

★   ★   ★

Bill kicked the plaster on his ankle with his good foot, serving only to stub his toe. If he

225

hadn't been such a goddamn fool and crippled himself just before she arrived — well, things might have been very different. He had liked her on sight, even though at first they seemed to have moved farther apart by meeting than they had been as cyber friends. But the day they had out together changed that and things were going well until she rocked the boat, and his world, by going to cat-sit or something for Fern Barclay. Now she had met up with that Adam fellow — whether by chance or design he didn't know, but suspected the latter. He felt annoyed with his daughter on several counts, not the least for bringing Adam here in the first place, for bringing to his notice that he was in Elmore and so was Eve, and most of all for being such a fool about Steve. Everyone except Chloe herself knew how Steve had always felt about her and he had strong suspicions that if Chloe let herself she would feel the same. Well, Adam was out of the way, Gary was going to marry Maureen, Steve had a clear run; Bill hoped he would use it. One person in the family stuffing up a relationship was more than enough, he reflected darkly.

Out in the paddock, Steve was doing his best. 'I hope you are not too upset about

Adam leaving?' he asked Chloe, looking for the cattle.

'Should I be?' Chloe sounded so uninterested that Steve believed her. 'They are under those gum trees.' She kicked Crispin into a trot.

'I was quite glad,' she admitted as they slowed down near the resting mob. 'I only asked him because I was sorry for him; he had nowhere to go for Christmas. It wasn't a good start being in bed with Eve.'

'What?'

'There was nothing wrong in it — at least I didn't think so at the time. He arrived much later than expected; I thought he must be coming the next morning. Eve and I had gone to bed. He claimed I misdirected him and he ended up in the wrong room and got into bed without putting the light on — that's what he said. I woke up when she screamed. I rushed in and found them in bed together. What's more, they were starkers. Do you think they did know one another before they got here?'

'You are adding two and two and making five at least. I liked Eve very much. I thought it was great that your father had found someone — it's pretty lonely for him.'

With a shrug Chloe gave her attention to herding the cattle towards the next paddock.

They worked in silence and when the gate was closed turned back towards the homestead. Steve felt irritation and frustration in a fifty-fifty mix rising within him and not trusting himself to speak hustled his horse into a canter and overtook her instead of jogging companionably at her side. When he realized that she was making no effort to catch up with him, he relented and reined in. He had known Chloe all her life and loved her for most of it; they had quarrelled before and always made it up, and no doubt they would again. But this time was different; he was running out of patience. If she took off back to Sydney or wherever again with nothing resolved between them he would just forget about her, he told himself. Only trouble was, could he?

He rode back in brooding silence, apparently unnoticed by Chloe, but when she turned round from throwing her saddle up on to the rack he was standing right behind her.

'Excuse me,' she said, with exaggerated politeness.

'Not till I have said what I have to say.'

Chloe raised her eyebrows and tried to move past him. Steve had never spoken to her in that tone of voice before; she felt a frisson of excitement and didn't know how close he was. 'Oh, and what may that be?' She tried to sound casual but could not keep the slight tremor out of her voice.

'Just this — Chloe McMahon, I have known you all our lives. I used to think of you as a very special sort of little sister. Things are different now; I don't think of you like that any more.' She raised her eyes to his face — it had suddenly occurred to her that she didn't think of him as a brother either — but lowered them when she saw how angry he looked. 'You are just a spoiled brat; you leave your father entirely on his own while you go and do your own thing, you couldn't care a stuff how he copes by himself, then you sail back with some fancy man in tow, find your father has found someone for himself and do your best to mess everything up for him. I don't like you much any more, but I do love you!' He stopped abruptly; nothing had come out the way he had meant it to. Exasperated, he put his hands on her shoulders. 'I could shake you!'

Chloe gasped, not because he had never touched her in anger before but because of the effect it was having on her. Her legs felt like jelly and her shoulders tingled under his hands. She registered the fact that he was now silent and dared to look up. Finding his gaze on her face, all these odd sensations were intensified. Slowly his hands moved down her arms, causing her to shudder involuntarily. He pulled her close and his lips claimed hers with the hunger of a man denied for far too long.

'That wasn't the way a brother should kiss his little sister,' Chloe protested weakly, coming up for air.

Steve grinned, his normal good humour restored. 'None of my sisters ever kissed me like that.' Then suddenly serious: 'I haven't felt in the least bit brotherly towards you for a long time. If the way you kissed me back then was a mistake on your part, say so now and I promise never to bother you again.'

She stared up into his face, knowing it was not a mistake; she wanted to kiss him like that again and again. How had she been so blind for so long? How could she ever have given a thought to anyone else, much less wasted a single heartbeat on them?

'You said I was spoilt.' It wouldn't do to capitulate too quickly.

'So I did. But I will overlook that, if you will. However . . . ' His voice was mock stern. 'I would like to know whether I am expected to be a brother or something else.'

She moved closer in the circle of his arms and her eyes searched his face. 'Something else, please, if that is what you really want.' The last few words were lost in a kiss that was even less fraternal than the last.

One look at their faces as they climbed the veranda steps hand in hand and Bill knew that his stubborn and apparently blind daughter had come to her senses at last and grabbed both her future and her happiness with both hands. It was stupid to allow his own sense of loss to cloud his happiness for them.

'The bemused expression on your faces leads me to ask; do we open the champagne?'

'Do we have any, Dad?'

'Well, no, we don't — but we can find something to drink your health.'

'Before we do that, may I have your daughter's hand, Mr McMahon?' Steve tried to look serious.

Bill smiled. 'It would appear you already have it.' They were indeed standing in front of him hand in hand. He smiled at Chloe. 'Come and give your old dad a kiss then see what we have in the drinks cupboard.'

'Stop being pathetic — you are not old.' Chloe kissed him lightly on the cheek. 'We have a sparkling white, not chilled but we can throw some ice cubes in and drink more to make up for the dilution.'

Acknowledging her father's raised glass, Chloe felt a stab of guilt. He looked certainly not old but forlorn. She remembered how she had suggested to him that Eve had something going with Adam. 'Dad,' she began tentatively, 'there is something I feel I should say about Eve — '

'I don't want to hear,' Bill interrupted. 'I made a mistake but it is behind me — let it stay there.'

'But Dad . . . '

'No, Chloe. I have told you, that episode in my life is over. Now, come on, let's finish this bottle.'

17

But Eve could not put Bill behind her. Too late she realized she had lost the nicest man she had ever met, and what for? Two weeks stuck on her own in a strange country. But he doesn't make my heart go 'zing', she thought, then chided herself for behaving like an immature schoolgirl instead of a mature woman. She reminded herself that she was middle-aged, a grandmother. Bill was older, but he was a man and had no biological clock to remind him.

In an effort to 'be her age', she was on a bus travelling down to Melbourne for the day, acting on a resolve to see something of Australia other than this small corner of Victoria. At Heathcote they picked up more passengers; it looked like a pleasant little town, although the main street must have been one of the longest in the country. She was tempted to abandon the bus and get out, to walk its length and enjoy window-shopping.

In Melbourne she regretted that she had not given into the whim. Big cities, she decided, were better experienced in company.

She had not felt so alone since she first arrived in Australia and found it a relief to board the bus for the return trip.

She let herself into the cottage and assured a protesting and hungry cat that she would attend to its needs immediately if not before, but her good intention was put on hold by the phone. As she approached it she noticed the flashing light of the answering service. Probably callers for Fern who did not realize she was away. She picked up the receiver, expecting another such call.

'Where on earth have you been?'

She tried hard not to be annoyed by Alex's proprietorial tone. 'I've been to Melbourne.'

'Melbourne? What on earth for?' He couldn't have sounded more astonished if she had said Mars.

'To have a look at it — be a tourist. Like you suggested.'

'I have been leaving messages on that damned answer machine, but got no response.'

'I've just told you I was out. So I couldn't answer.' She tried hard not to lose her temper. 'Did you want me for anything important?'

'To ask you to have lunch with me — now you are home you can make it dinner.'

'How kind of you, Alex, but no. It has been

234

a tiring day and I am only just home and Boss is clamouring to be fed.' All of which were true.

'You are standing me up for that bloody cat!'

Eve managed a laugh as if he were joking, but she was sure he was not.

'Yes,' she told him, 'the cat and a hot bath and an early night.'

'I shall call you in the morning, arrange lunch or something . . . ' He sounded pained. 'Goodnight,' he added grudgingly.

'Goodnight — and thanks!' Eve responded listlessly, wondering what she was thanking him for. She was truly exhausted, Boss was circling her legs demanding, in his rather strident voice, to be fed, and the idea of a relaxing bath grew ever more enticing. A short while later, wallowing in the fragrant steam created by a generous handful of the lavender bath crystals temptingly displayed in a glass jar, she wondered why she didn't find it flattering to be the object of Alex's attention. He was clever, amusing (most of the time), and undeniably good to look at, but he didn't make her pulse race and she sometimes found him confident to the point of arrogance. Perhaps, she thought gloomily, the fault was with herself; perhaps she was beyond that sort of thing. As if to contradict this thought, she remembered Adam and their surreal meeting: suppose, just suppose, instead of screaming her head off she had remained silent and reached her hands out to draw his naked body closer to her own. She surrendered to erotic fancies till the cooling water and her rumbling stomach urged her to get out and search for something to eat.

⋆ ⋆ ⋆

Chloe switched on the bedside light and reached for her book. She was feeling a tad guilty about telling her father that she had seen Adam driving up to Fern's house. She shouldn't, she knew, have let him think there was anything significant about it. She wished he had listened when she tried to put things right. Steve, she knew, would tell her that she must make him listen. He liked Eve and thought she was just what her father needed. She closed her book and replaced it on the bedside table — it couldn't be much good, she thought, as it failed to take her attention from her somewhat uncomfortable thoughts. Promising herself that in the morning she would have another go at putting things straight with her father, she let her thoughts drift to Steve: how on earth could she have been so stupid for so long and imagined for one instant that there was anyone else in the world for her? On this thought and a sigh of satisfaction, she slid back into sleep.

Sleep did not come so easily to Bill. He had known Steve all his life and loved him as if he were his own son, so when they walked in hand in hand he felt happy almost to the point of tears. He had known for a long time how Steve felt and knew Chloe could never find a better man, so it had been a real blow when she had asked that fellow Adam for Christmas. He had grieved for Steve then; now it seemed that he should be sorry for himself. If everything he heard was true, Adam had now taken up with Eve. Having Adam and Eve together, had been, he reflected with an upsurge of his usual wry humour, a recipe for disaster. On that thought he determined to stop thinking about Eve in any context. He swore aloud as, in his efforts to get comfortable, he stubbed his toe on the plaster cast. Thank God the damn thing would be off soon. With the best will in the world he could not keep his thoughts away from Eve. Their cyber friendship had been a real meeting of minds, unencumbered by physical attraction, till he met her. He finally dropped to sleep, his undisciplined thoughts full of Eve.

Eve woke up knowing she must contact Bill

and try and make him see why she had taken up Fern's offer. She dialled the McMahons' number before her wavering courage died and while the jug boiled for her first coffee of the day. A caffeine hit she needed *now*, she thought, her heart beating in sync with the brrr-brrr of the phone.

'Hello!' Chloe sounded breathless and Eve imagined her rushing in from her outside chores.

'Chloe — hello, it's me, Eve. Is — is your father there?' Eve, fresh from bed, sounded equally breathless.

'Er . . . um . . . I — I think so — I . . . ' Chloe stammered, frantically beckoning to her father, who shook his head vehemently. 'Just a minute — I'll — I'll see if I can find him . . . ' Covering the mouthpiece with her hand, she hissed at Bill, 'Dad, come and speak to Eve — please!'

His response was to turn his back on her and hobble away towards his bedroom, unaware that the sound of his crutches was audible on the other end of the line.

'I'm sorry, Eve, I — I can't find him. Shall I — Can I give him a message?'

'Oh — just tell him I rang.' How far away could a man with a plaster on his leg get?

Eve's flat voice, with its undertone of hurt and rejection, touched Chloe's conscience. In her newfound happiness she wished the same for everyone. 'He's probably on his way out to the car — he hopes to get the plaster off today. I'm driving him to the hospital in a minute.'

'Wish him well from me, then — I won't hold you up.' Eve swallowed past the lump in her throat.

Chloe found her father sitting on his bed, gazing into space. 'You should have spoken to her. I felt very uncomfortable lying to her.'

Bill shrugged, feigning lack of interest. 'Are you ready to leave? I don't want to spend the whole day at the hospital.'

★　★　★

Eve turned away from the phone, her shoulders slumped. If that was how he felt . . . She straightened up, turned to the boiling jug and made a strong cup of coffee. She told herself she didn't care, but when the phone rang a few minutes later she sprang to answer it so quickly she almost spilled her coffee, hoping Bill had really been unavailable.

'Good morning, Eve.'

'Hello, Alex.' She was relieved to note that her voice sounded normal.

'Lunch today?' She remembered he had said something about it the previous evening.

'You can't tell me you have had a better offer between talking to me last night and now.'

'No, I can't — and I wasn't going to. In fact, if that is an invitation, I accept.' After Bill's rejection, it was balm to be wanted.

'Would you like me to pick you up and we will go off somewhere or would you prefer to come here? Fiona always leaves a well-stocked freezer.'

Eve, already regretting her brittle acceptance of his invitation, didn't particularly want to do either. Just suppose she had been wrong. After all, if Chloe had told her the truth then there was always the chance that when Chloe gave Bill her message he might call her back. 'Why don't you come here for lunch? It is after all my turn to host you.' In her desire to be under no obligation to Alex, she forgot that he might read more into her invitation than she intended.

'Is noon too early?'

'That will be fine.'

A cursory review of fridge and pantry told her that she would have to go out and shop even though she had no plans for a large gourmet lunch. Omelette and salad preceded by soup and followed by coffee, cheese and biscuits. Alex had a way of rubbing her up the wrong way.

The bottles of wine in each hand and

absence of any phone calls helped to warm her to him when she opened the door on the stroke of midday.

'I didn't know which you would prefer — or what we were going to eat — so I brought a choice, one red, one white,' Alex explained as he placed them both on the bench. 'If you want the white, it needs chilling . . . ' He looked round vaguely. 'Does Fern have a wine chiller?'

'I am afraid it is a very simple lunch.' Eve cursed herself for sounding apologetic. 'Soup, omelettes and salad, so I think the red.'

Eve was feeling mellow and relaxed after two glasses of the red wine, which was excellent — a local vintage, Alex had told her. She had her back to him getting the coffee when he asked what her plans were.

'What are you going to do when Fern gets back?'

'I haven't really thought,' Eve admitted. 'I would like to see a bit more of the country but — I don't know — I may go back to England.'

'You have several choices: see more of Australia, head back to England or even return to the McMahons'. How long did you plan to stay when you came?'

'Would you like coffee?' Eve stalled to hide her indecision.

'Yes, please, I would like coffee. You must have had some idea,' Alex persisted.

'Not really. I came out on a sudden whim, and an open-ended ticket.' She didn't want to say 'at Bill's invitation'.

'Throwing out casual invitations seems to be a family failing according to Adam.' Alex looked up from the coffee he was stirring with a faintly malicious smile.

There seemed little else to say but 'Yes.' She felt her cheeks warming, hoping that Adam, while gossiping to Alex, had not regaled him with the story of their first meeting. Alex, she knew, had a way of getting things out of people. That irritating half-smile still played on the corners of his mouth.

'You said you were a good little girl.'

What did it matter to Alex — or anyone else, for that matter — what sort of a child she had been? 'I was,' she admitted. 'My father was strict so I didn't have much option. I was also a good teenager, a good wife and a good mother, as you established when we had this conversation last time.' Eve flushed at the faintly mocking tone in his voice. 'Do I gather that you equate 'good' with dull and ordinary?'

'Not at all.' Alex's smile was urbane but Eve felt anger like a rising tide, causing her to flush. She stood up abruptly and gathered up their dishes, then took them over to the sink.

'Whatever made you up sticks and come to Australia?' he enquired of her back.

Suddenly very angry, she spun round and faced him. 'Whatever you are implying or want to know, I don't like it, I don't like it one bit. So if — '

'I can't believe you are going to tell me to leave,' Alex cut in. As that was exactly what she had been about to say, she managed a rueful laugh instead. At least he had saved her from a breach of good manners.

He gave a shrug, denoting helplessness, which Eve did not believe in one bit. 'As a psychologist I am always interested in people and what makes them tick.'

'Well, there is nothing in the least interesting about me. I am just a very ordinary woman, not an 'interesting case' at all.'

'To me no one is ordinary, and I find you very interesting — not as a case but as a person. I feel there are hidden depths beneath your quiet, well-behaved exterior. After all, coming out here to meet a man you hardly knew was, well, shall we say anything but ordinary.'

'Actually, I think it was very ordinary. I am sure people are doing it all the time nowadays — they meet in cyber space and international travel is so easy and fast that they can meet up with each other as soon as think about it.'

'Or without thinking about it much?'

'Alex . . . ' Eve banged the plates they had been using down on the draining board with more vigour than was strictly necessary. 'If you want someone to psychoanalyse then please go and find someone else.'

'My dear Eve . . . ' She winced as he said this. 'Can't you forget my profession for a while and see me as a friend?'

'Can't *you* forget you are a psychologist for five minutes, Alex, and see me as a friend?'

'I see you as a very attractive woman — with hidden depths.'

'There you go again. I have told you I am very ordinary — what you see is what you get.' Alex, she was well aware, was far from ordinary himself. From their first meeting she had never been sure whether she liked him or not. She was beginning to think not. Clever, even charismatic, but, she decided, a user — his books no doubt the result of conversations like this with other gullible people.

'My hidden depths are so well hidden, if they exist, I do not know about them myself but I am certainly quite out of my depth in this conversation, so please change it.'

'You haven't told me what you are planning

244

to do next. Where will you go when Fern reclaims her house?'

'I haven't told you because I haven't decided. I would like to see a bit more of Australia before I leave — forever probably. I don't know — I really don't.'

'Why should going back mean you will never return?'

Eve 'tcched' in exasperation. 'Because it is a very long way indeed, and quite expensive. When I get back to England I shall have to think about earning a living.' A small sigh was wrung out of her at the prospect.

'I suppose you have family in England?'

'You are still making this conversation sound as if you are subjecting me to the third degree. Yes, I have a married daughter, a son-in-law, a new grandchild and . . . ' Her voice faded out. You couldn't count a divorced husband married to someone else.

'What work did you do before you were married — afterwards — any time — what did you do? What sort of a job would you be looking for?' Alex asked, his voice tinged with impatience.

'I was a secretary. I would probably need to take a computer course before I could get a decent job,' Eve admitted. 'They were pretty thin on the ground when I was in the workforce before.'

'I need a secretary,' Alex pointed out, looking at her, she thought, like a farmer assessing a likely piece of livestock. 'Or you could marry me?'

Eve had read about people being 'lost for words'. Now she knew exactly what the phrase meant.

'Of course you are joking,' she finally stammered.

'No. I am perfectly serious.'

For a moment Eve allowed herself to give his suggestion credence. Undoubtedly it would solve most of her problems: whether to go or stay, what to do if she stayed, what to do if she returned to England. Then reality, or sanity, clicked in and pointed out to her that it would probably create a lot more problems than it solved. Marriage to Alex would not be easy even if one were in love with him. She was not. She was attracted to him, a little, liked him sporadically, and for the rest of the time was either indifferent to him or disliked him. 'W-what are you doing?' Eve fought the quaver in her voice as, without warning, he bounded across the room towards her.

'I had in mind a kiss — to see how we both felt about it.'

'Oh!' The quaver became a squeak.

'Is that so outrageous that you have to sound like an elderly virgin about to be ravished?'

He held her gaze for a moment then turned away. Eve, to her chagrin, felt only disappointment.

'Were you serious?' She broke the silence hesitantly.

'Very. I need a secretary and I am prepared to marry you, if that is the only way I can get a good one.'

'You make it sound like a business proposition.'

'But that is the best basis for a successful relationship: fair exchange. You get a job and a home and the chance to live here permanently, I get the services of a first class secretary.'

Eve thought it a cynical proposition. There had been no mention of love.

'I suppose you would like love too? That comes later, with luck. Most of what precipitates couples into marriage is lust. Eventually, if they have common interests, maybe working together for the same goal, when they enjoy one another's company, without sex, then love is born and a lasting bond formed.'

'Doesn't romance come into it at all?'

'Romance is a figment of the imagination.'

He dismissed the idea as absurd with one of his inimitable shrugs. 'Sleep on it — I'll give you twenty-four hours. The offer of a job as my secretary still stands, even if you reject marriage.'

'Thank you,' Eve murmured, annoyed with her own meek humility, but he was already out the door and anyway, what else was there to say?

As she let the water out of the sink, she decided that Alex Cameron was quite, quite mad. All the same, his offer of a job was tempting. She was already beginning to love Australia, but could she love Alex Cameron?

The afternoon stretched ahead of her with nothing special to do and no company but her own. Boss had wandered off into the garden and was taking a prolonged siesta somewhere in the shade. He had the right idea, she thought, as a huge yawn overtook her. She wandered into the bedroom and flopped down on top of the doona, intending to give intelligent thought to Alex's proposition, but it was too hot for serious thought and her lids drooped then closed as sleep overtook her.

She was roused from a totally confusing dream in which the three men who had featured prominently in her life since her arrival in Australia — Adam, Bill and Alex

248

— were dancing round her in a circle, chanting something she could not distinguish, and in the distance she could see the figure of her ex-husband vanishing into a swirling white mist. She struggled to a sitting position, feeling utterly disorientated and wondering where the persistently ringing bell was coming from. By the time she had worked out it was the telephone, struggled off the bed and staggered out of the room, it had stopped.

'Damn!' she cursed as she dropped into a chair at the table and pushed her hair back from her forehead in an attempt to reorientate herself. 'Probably someone after Fern,' she muttered aloud, and didn't bother to check on the number that had called. She shook her head as if she could shake off the memory of the confusing dream. She had no intention of asking Alex for an interpretation.

Alex! 'Oh, God!' she groaned aloud and wondered if she could make her escape somewhere before she had to face him next day and tell him her decision. She walked across the kitchen and switched on the jug to make a cup of tea. She was still English enough to see a nice cuppa as the antidote to all trials and tribulations. By the time she was sipping it she had convinced herself that he hadn't really meant what he said. It was too bizarre to propose to someone on so little acquaintance and it would be even more so to accept. Maybe she had been dreaming then — or simply misunderstood what he had said.

Even the tea did not stop the feeling of disorientation she felt, the result not only of being woken suddenly but dropping asleep in the middle of the day. The dream hadn't helped either. A sudden memory flashed into her mind of Alex asking her if she dreamed here in the cottage and when she said no, telling her that Fern did. She didn't for one moment think that bricks and mortar could make one dream, but certainly one's inner fears and worries could. She was getting morbid and introverted; a walk might clear her head. Briefly she wished Boss were a dog not a cat, if only to give her a reason to walk and provide company.

She walked past the newsagent and bought a paper. That provided a reason; walking along with a paper in her hand, it was obvious why she was out. As she realized the way her thoughts were going, she almost stopped in her tracks. *She did not need a reason.* She was a grown woman and was at perfect liberty to walk when and where she wished. She could also, if she so desired, marry Alex, or anyone else for that matter, without asking anyone's permission or worrying what other people thought. She recalled a saying she had seen somewhere and stored in the recesses of her mind to bring out and polish when she needed it. One of those times had been when she made the decision to visit Australia, another was now. '*They say — What do they say? — Let them say.*' Eve repeated the words in her head, twice for good measure.

By the time she put the key in the cottage door, she had come to a decision. To take the job with Alex and nothing else. She had switched on the answering service and it was flashing now with, she guessed, another message for Fern. Suspecting it might be Alex already pressing for an answer, she didn't replay the message immediately. When she did her breath caught in her throat. It was Bill's voice speaking to her.

'I hope you listen to this, Eve, and don't assume it is for Fern. Maybe you could call me back on my mobile?'

Eve picked up the receiver to dial then stopped with it in mid-air; she didn't know his mobile number. She played the message again, in case he had given it and she had stopped the playback too soon. He had either assumed she knew it or forgotten to give it. She began to dial his fixed phone number, then her mind went blank; she couldn't remember it. Desperately she thumbed through the telephone directory, grateful his name wasn't Smith — at least McMahon did not come by the page, just a column or so.

'Hello . . . ' Eve felt a sharp stab of disappointment when Chloe answered the phone. 'Is — is B . . . your father there?' she asked hesitantly.

'No, sorry, he is out somewhere in the car. Is that Eve?'

'In the car? But I thought — I mean — his ankle?' Eve stammered.

'Oh, he had the plaster off this morning. I didn't think he would be able to drive but he insisted he could. They bound it up for him till it gets its normal strength back. I made sure he took his mobile phone with him so that he could get in touch with me if necessary.'

'I wonder — Could you — Do you have his number?'

'Yeah, sure.' Without hesitation, Chloe rattled the number off. Eve scribbled it down and read it back to make sure she had it correct.

'Thanks very much, Chloe. Bye.' Eve replaced the receiver quickly before Chloe could ask her why she wanted it. She was slightly surprised to find there was a tremor in her fingers as she dialled.

'Eve?' His voice sounded taut; was he

annoyed with her?

'Hello, Bill — sorry I have been a bit of a long time getting back to you. I didn't have your mobile number. I had to call Chloe and get it from her. Luckily she was in and answered the phone immediately . . . ' Eve knew she was gabbling and was relieved when he interrupted her when she had to pause for breath.

'Can I come and see you? I — feel we — need to talk.'

'Yes, yes, of course. When — ' She was about to ask when he intended to come or at least how long he would be when, with a curt 'Good — see you soon,' the line went dead. Eve stood for a second looking vaguely at the silent instrument in her hand before putting it carefully in its rest. He had sounded so abrupt — almost angry — but what had she done? Surely he couldn't still be smarting about the last time they had spoken to each other and she had been so hasty? She put up her hand to her untidy hair, remembered that she hadn't even looked at her face since before she went out for her walk and dashed into the bedroom to run a comb through her hair and quickly dab on some lipstick. As a last thought she sprayed perfumed cologne on her throat just as a car drew up outside.

Eve stood at the window and watched Bill get out. He moved slowly and carefully and pulled a stick out, looked at it disdainfully, threw it back in the car then reached inside and drew it out again. From the movement of his shoulders she guessed he was sighing in resignation and exasperation. She smiled softly to herself, surprised how very glad she was to see him, then watched him walk carefully up the path to the door, leaning on the stick and limping slightly. She opened the door as he reached it. 'Hello!' they both spoke in unison, then Eve pulled the door wide. 'Come in!' she invited with a sweeping gesture.

Bill let his eyes run round the room and she could see that he liked what he saw. Eve hoped the same applied to her. 'It — it's good to see you walking again. Do sit down.' As she spoke, the oddity of asking him to sit down immediately after telling him she was pleased to see him walking struck her.

The same thought must have crossed Bill's mind for he answered with a rueful grin, 'So good that you want me to stop doing it? Actually, you have never seen me walking on my own two legs, have you?'

Eve smiled, enjoying this confirmation of their like-minded thinking and humour. 'No,

I haven't — that probably makes me all the more pleased to see you doing it so well.'

'I still depend on this darn stick,' he grumbled as he dropped down on to the couch. 'But I haven't come here to talk about how well I can or cannot walk, but to straighten things out between us. I feel I may owe you an apology. I will know when you have given me an explanation.' He glowered and Eve felt her heart sink. What had she to explain — and could she?

18

'I should have spoken to you when you telephoned. It was feeble of me to make Chloe say I wasn't there.'

'It was,' Eve agreed. 'Anyway, I could hear your crutches. Would you like a cup of tea or coffee?'

'Whatever you are making.' He felt slightly put out; it was never good being caught in a lie.

He didn't feel any better when she added, 'I was ringing you to apologize.' He probably didn't care, she thought, if all he thought needed mending between them was the fact that he had refused to speak to her.

'What have you to apologize for?'

Eve thought he sounded as if she might have something. But he continued, 'I am sorry I spoke to you as I did. Even sorrier I let you go without getting things straight. The thing was . . .' he tried to explain without implicating Chloe. 'Well, I thought you had arranged to meet Adam here.' The last words came in a rush.

'Oh, no!' Eve protested. 'I had no idea he was here. Why on earth should you think I had arranged to meet him, or even wanted to?' She began to say that he was Chloe's friend and of no interest to her, but Bill was fumbling in his pocket. He handed a crumpled slip of paper to her. 'Can you explain this?'

Eve recognized the note Adam had slid under her door. 'How did you get it?' she asked, her voice toneless.

'Chloe found it on your bedroom floor after you left.'

'I see — and as Adam belonged to her she was justifiably annoyed. I have no idea why he did such a stupid thing. There was not — ever — anything between Adam and me and if you think so then — well, I am sorry. Adam was Chloe's friend.' Her voice grew tight and she was shocked to feel tears pricking behind her lids. He had come to confront her, not apologize.

'Not any more.' Bill sounded jubilant and when she looked up she saw he was smiling.

'What — what do you mean?'

'She and Steve are now what, in today's jargon, I believe is known as an item.'

'Oh, Bill — I am so glad!' Eve was genuinely delighted, on her own account as well as for Chloe. 'Anyone with half an eye could see how he felt about her — anyone it seemed but Chloe. I knew she really cared for him right from the moment I arrived.'

'How come?'

'She didn't seem to like the idea one bit of him meeting me at the station. She didn't believe I didn't know he existed till I stepped off the train at Bendigo and had come at your invitation. Because you hadn't mentioned me she jumped to the wrong conclusion. Then there was that silly incident with Adam.'

Bill believed her, but all the same wished she hadn't mentioned that.

The jug had boiled and switched itself off. 'Did you want coffee or tea?' Eve repeated as she flicked it back on.

'Oh, tea, please.' She was, he could see, determined he had something.

'Tea for two coming up.'

Her smile was warm as she placed a small tray on an occasional table in front of the couch. She straightened up and looked at him thoughtfully. 'You look heaps better,' she assured him. She had almost said younger but bowed to tact and changed it.

'You, too.' How much more attractive and vibrant she appeared than the wan, pale woman he had first met. 'You have acquired an Australian tan and it suits you.'

'Thanks, Bill. I was thinking much the same about you. Not about the Australian tan — because of course you have always had that — but how much better you look.'

Realizing she had already said that, she quickly added, 'It must be a great relief to have that plaster off and you will find your ankle gets stronger every day. I can remember breaking my ankle a few years back. I was so disappointed when the plaster came off to find it was still so weak, but in an incredibly short time it was back to normal.'

'It was such a stupid thing to happen. I would have stopped you coming but I knew it was too late; you would already be on the plane.'

'I'm very glad you didn't. I have enjoyed my visit so much,' Eve said quietly as she poured his tea, surprising him by remembering just how he liked it without asking.

'You sound as if you are about to leave.'

'I can't stay for ever.' But she could, if he asked her. She remembered Alex. Had she let him think she might stay for him?

'Eve, I am so sorry about the things I said.' There was no point in sashaying round it — he might as well come straight out and just say Sorry.

'I am sorry, too, Bill, really sorry. I said some stupid things too. How about we both forget it. Least said soonest mended, don't you think?'

His face lit up. 'Let's try and start at the beginning, shall we? Pretend we are meeting face to face for the first time and I have two good legs!'

Eve smiled at him. 'If you like — but there are some things I don't want to forget. Our day in Daylesford, for instance. I enjoyed that so much, Bill. And your leg — well, don't you think you are making too much of it? After all, we became very close friends when, to all intents and purposes, neither of us had any body at all, so why should one ankle out of use make any difference?'

Pushing away his teacup, Bill got to his feet, moved the small table out of the way and stood in front of her; 'Stand up, Eve,' he commanded. Obediently she did as he asked and looked at him with a slight frown of bewilderment. 'It made a difference because I couldn't stand straight in front of you without those damn crutches and take you in my arms, like this.' Suiting the action to the words, he put his arms round her and drew her close enfolding her to his heart.

Slowly Eve relaxed against him; she could feel something beating between them but had no idea whether it was his heart or her own, or even the two beating in unison. Then she turned her face up to his, noting as she had when she first met him the brilliant blue of his eyes. 'Bill?' she whispered before his lips met hers and effectively stopped any further questions.

It was a moment before she relaxed completely and gave herself up to the sensations that were invading her body, and then it was as if a match had been touched to a flare as all her senses leapt to meet his. It was a long time since she had been kissed by anyone. She dismissed Alex's kiss as 'not serious' and never had she felt her whole body respond like this; from the tips of her toes to the top of her head, she was totally aware of him. When the need for air finally drew them apart, they stayed quite still, looking into one another's eyes. 'That was worth waiting for,' Bill said softly. 'Somehow I knew you would be a wonderful kisser.'

Eve laughed softly at the compliment. 'No one has ever said that to me before,' she admitted, 'but then no one has ever kissed me quite like that before either.'

Holding her hand, Bill drew her back to the couch. 'Sit down and talk to me.' He patted the cushion at his side. 'Absurd though it seems, we communicated much more with each other when you were in England and I was here in Australia,' he complained.

Eve looked up at him with a mischievous sidelong smile. 'Then maybe I had better hurry back to England.'

'That's what I want to discuss with you.' Bill sounded so serious that Eve felt a momentary pang of alarm.

'You — you don't want me to stay?'

'Eve — Oh, Eve . . . ' Bill put his arm round her shoulders and hugged her to him in the sort of comforting gesture one might give a child. 'Why ever should you think I would want you to go? I want you here — with me — more than anything in the world. I was just reverting to my practical farmer persona, assuming that it would be difficult, if not impossible, for you to stay on now. You must have things to settle back in England — a life there to wind up before you embark on a new one here.'

'I suppose so,' Eve murmured in a forlorn little voice. Was he softening his rejection of her to be kind?

'Don't look so dejected — like I said, I was just being practical. I guess I should have been romantic instead?' He turned her round towards him and tilted her chin so that she was forced to look into his face. 'I love you, Eve. Is it too much to hope that you may care — just a little — for me?'

Eve gulped, and then blinked her eyes before refocusing them on his face. A face that she realized had become very dear to her. It wasn't startlingly goodlooking like that of

Alex, or even Adam, but it was the face she had grown to love. There was living and loving etched on it in the fine lines round his eyes and mouth, she liked his silvering hair and of course his brilliant blue eyes, but most of all she liked the way he looked at her and smiled at her. She could not remember anyone ever looking at her before with so much tenderness. It made her want to weep or laugh or hug him as tightly as she could, but she did none of these, just nodded, then absurdly shook her head. Realizing that she was offering him a very confused answer, she stammered, 'Yes — I mean no — it's not too much to hope at all!'

'Then you will marry me?' Bill asked anxiously. 'I'm old-fashioned enough to want you to.'

'And I'm old-fashioned enough to want to.'

'Does that mean your answer is yes?'

Eve nodded. 'I guess so. Will Chloe mind?' Eve asked tentatively, thinking that her own family in England would probably have some scathing comments when they learned their mother planned to marry someone they had never heard of on the other side of the world. They knew nothing of her deepening friendship with Bill over the last year; did not even know he existed. But they were hurdles she would meet when she came to them. As far as they were concerned, it was crazy enough of her to spend her small legacy on a holiday in Australia, of all places. They would be convinced she had really flipped her lid when she told them she intended to marry Bill and spend the rest of her life here.

Bill laughed. 'Chloe will probably be delighted, but if she did mind it wouldn't make a scrap of difference to me. This is my life — yours and mine — and not hers. But what about your family — will they mind?'

'I have to confess that my daughter does not know of your existence,' she admitted, somewhat shamefaced. 'She will probably think I have taken total leave of my senses and may regret the loss of a handy baby-sitter but, like you said, this is our life now, yours and mine.'

'You will come back to the farm?'

Eve nodded, almost too happy to speak.

'Tonight — with me?' Bill pressed.

She nodded again, then remembered and shook her head. 'No, Bill, I'm sorry, I can't. I promised Fern I'd look after her house and her cat — particularly her cat. I can't possibly walk out and leave him.'

'Do you mean that unprepossessing black and white creature?' he asked, feigning incredulity. 'You are telling me he takes precedence over me?'

Eve looked anxious until she saw the twinkle in his eyes and realized he was teasing her. 'I'm afraid so — in this instance,' she told him.

Bill heaved an exaggerated sigh. 'In that case I shall have to ask you if you will put me up for the night.'

'I think that might be arranged,' Eve told him demurely. As she looked up and their eyes met, so much flowed between them — the friendship and understanding built up in their long Internet friendship plus that extra something that only personal contact could give to their relationship. She was sure, somehow, that in Bill she had found what every woman wanted in her heart, a man who would see her truly as a person, not as a wife. They would be equals and partners in the truest sense of the word. She didn't know how to explain this and instead said, 'Your darn leg wasn't the cause of our difficulties, but how you felt about it was, and we were so seldom alone together; we needed to get to know each other in a different way from our Internet friendship.' She smiled. '*You* had a problem with your leg, and I don't mean physical — you were so convinced that it had upset all our plans that it sort of got in the way of us really getting to know one another.'

'It certainly did!' Bill agreed.

'I meant mentally, not physically,' Eve pointed out when she caught the glint in his eyes and saw his lips twitch. What a relief it was, she thought, to find that he really was the man she had thought he would be over their long friendship in cyberspace.

The rest of the day slid by in talk; easy conversation recapping what they had already learned about each other over the past year. In the evening they went out for a drink that ended in dinner and strolled back to the cottage hand in hand through the soft Australian night.

'I suppose it is bitterly cold at home now,' Eve mused.

'England, you mean?'

She looked at him in surprise. 'Of course I mean England — that's where I came from, remember?'

'You still call it home — somehow I thought Australia would be home from now on.'

'Oh, Bill, don't split hairs. I suppose in one way England will always be home to me. After all, it is where I was born and raised and where I have lived all my life — till now.'

He pulled her close as they stepped inside the cottage and closed the door behind them. 'Of course, my darling, but let's not look back — instead look to our future together.' Eve nodded and mumbled something affirmative, her mind registering the fact that he had called her 'darling' for the first time as his lips claimed hers, effectively silencing both of them.

Bill shook his head vigorously when she asked if he would like a hot drink or anything. 'I don't know what 'anything' implies but I'll take a chance on it,' he told her as he gently but firmly steered her towards the bedroom.

Eve watched him undress, overwhelmed by reluctance to take her own clothes off. Acutely aware that while his own body was trim and sinewy as befitted a man who spent so much active time outdoors, he might think hers decidedly past its use-by date. He was standing before her almost naked before she slowly began to remove her clothes, painfully aware that her waist was not as trim as it had once been and that her body was laced with stretchmarks. She lowered her eyes and turned away from his gaze.

'What is the matter, Eve?' He asked softly. 'If you don't want this, we don't have to.'

'No — no — it's just that . . . ' The last thing she wanted to do was wound him with rejection. 'It's my . . . ' she began haltingly.

'Your body is beautiful,' he said softly.

'Don't add 'for your age',' she said, smiling, warmed by his words.

'I promise not to — if you don't say it to me.' He grinned and stepped forward. 'Come here, woman . . . ' Before she knew what was happening, he had swept her up in his arms and carried her over to the bed, where he laid her down gently and leaned over her supporting his weight with his hands.

Eve found her breath coming raggedly and felt a warm glow stealing over her body. She reached her own arms up, locked them round his neck and pulled him down on top of her.

Their union was just that; a fusion not only of two bodies but it seemed of two souls. Eve had no inkling that it could be like this and when she curved her body into his afterwards and fell asleep with her head against his shoulder, she felt utterly at peace and knew that from this moment on when she talked of 'home' it would simply mean the place where he was.

★   ★   ★

They probably wouldn't have got up all day if hunger hadn't driven them to the kitchen. Eve was there sorting out breakfast things, dressed in the light travelling robe she had brought with her, when there was a vigorous knock on the door. She would have taken the coward's way and not opened it if she had realized who it was.

'Alex!' she exclaimed, automatically pulling the robe closer across her breasts.

His glance was a blend of admiration, surprise and reluctant apology. 'Sorry to be so early . . . ' His voice trailed off as he registered her less than enthusiastic expression. 'You know, I am not really so early — it seems to me you are rather late. I never thought of you as a late riser somehow.'

'I'm not — I don't — I usually . . . ' Eve stammered wildly. She had entirely forgotten until this moment that Alex had said he expected her answer this morning — but he hadn't said he would come round and collect it. She would have liked to slam the door in his face and pretend he wasn't there, but even if her innate good manners had allowed such behaviour it would have been difficult, for he had his foot in the doorway.

'Is there any chance of a coffee?' he asked.

Again she would liked to have said no but apart from anything else the enticing aroma of percolating coffee was just beginning to fill the air, accompanied by the steady burp, burp of Fern's percolator. Reluctantly, Eve opened the door a bit further and stepped back. At the precise moment that Alex followed her into the house, Bill called out from the bathroom, 'There is a man's towelling robe on the door — would anyone mind if I borrowed it?'

'Go ahead,' Alex called before Eve could gather her wits sufficiently to answer. There was silence from the bathroom and Eve could imagine Bill stunned for a moment at hearing a male voice answer his query. Then he appeared, still knotting the tie round his waist, and faced Alex. The two men stared at one another, heads slightly jutting forward. For a wild moment Eve suppressed a desire to laugh — they looked so absurdly like a couple of roosters trying to outface each other prior to a fight.

'What are you doing here?' they demanded in unison.

To Eve's surprise it was Bill who recovered his sangfroid first to answer, somewhat truculently, 'I should have thought that was obvious — what about you?'

Alex threw Eve a withering look. 'It is all too obvious you two have been enjoying a night in each other's company. That being so, I have no need to get an answer to the question I left with Eve yesterday and my presence here is quite superfluous.' With that he turned on his heel and made for the door, turning round just before he left to say in an icy tone, 'Continue enjoying yourselves, please. Do not let my untimely appearance interrupt anything.'

As the door closed firmly behind him, Bill turned to Eve. 'What the hell was he doing here at this time in the morning? What did he mean? What question were you supposed to answer?'

Eve made a great show of busily setting breakfast things out, wondering what to say. First thing in the morning after spending the night with a man didn't seem quite the appropriate moment to tell him that the early-morning visitor had come to see if she intended to marry him.

'Eve!' Bill's voice rapped out. 'What was he here for and what did he want to know?'

The only thing to say appeared to be the truth, or maybe it was just too early in the morning to think up a convincing alternative, Eve thought, as she put toast and marmalade on the table and faced Bill. 'He came to see if I had decided to marry him.'

'He what?' Bill stared at her, aghast. 'What reason, what possible reason did he have to imagine you would? I think,' he continued in a deceptively calm and level voice, 'you have some explaining to do, Eve.' The thought flashed into his mind that maybe Chloe had been right in the first instance when she told him that she had seen Adam driving up to the cottage where Eve was staying. He looked at her, and remembered the night they had just spent in each other's arms: could he really believe that didn't mean anything to her? And yet why had Alex Cameron turned up on her doorstep this morning unless there had been some sort of an understanding between them?

Eve stared back at him, noting with some part of her brain that his bright blue eyes seemed to have lost some of their colour this morning and were cold as crystal. She shrugged helplessly and felt her shoulders droop as she half-turned away from him. 'I — I thought he was joking.' She spoke so quietly that her words were almost inaudible.

'It isn't something men usually joke about. I don't, anyway. Or did you perhaps think that about me too?' Bill demanded, his voice dry.

'No — no — of course not!' She turned to face him fully, tears suddenly brimming and her voice choked as she fought to maintain her composure.

'Was there — was there anything between you two?' He had to ask even though he hated himself for his lack of trust.

Eve shook her head vigorously. 'No — nothing. We — we went out once or twice, that was all. To tell you the truth, I found him a bit of a trial at times — he never stopped being a psychologist and I . . . ' Her voice trailed away as she realized that what she was saying was doing less than nothing to convince Bill.

'Are you going to tell me that you wanted him to stop being a psychologist and just be a man?' he asked sharply.

'No, I'm not — I'm not saying that at all — but if that is what you really think of me then there doesn't seem much future for us, does there?'

Bill stared at her; he couldn't believe this was really happening. All he wanted to do was step across the few feet of floor that separated them and take her in his arms and tell her how much he loved her and needed her. But he stood there, as if his feet were glued to the ground, and she just stared back at him, eyes tear-bright, mouth set in an angry, hurt line. They might have stood like this for ever if the phone hadn't startled them both.

'You had better answer it.' Bill nodded towards it.

'It is probably someone wanting Fern.' Eve waited for the answering service to click in. As almost all the calls were intended for Fern, she kept the machine on most of the time. Both of them started when they heard Chloe's voice and Bill moved towards it, thinking it must be some message for him and fearing that something had gone wrong on the farm. He stopped and Eve quickly grabbed the receiver when she heard Chloe's voice, taught with urgency, call her name.

'Eve? Are you there, Eve? If so, please pick up the phone. Eve — '

'Yes, yes, I am here, Chloe. What is the matter? If you — ' She was about to say that if she was worried about her father, there was no need because he was right here with her, but Chloe interrupted her.

'I'm so glad I caught you, Eve. There is a message on our answering service for you.'

'For me?' Eve wondered who on earth could be ringing her on the McMahons' number and why Chloe sounded agitated.

'It's from England — from your son-in-law, I think. Anyway, it says please call him back as soon as you possibly can. He left the number, but I guess you know it.'

'Yes, yes, I do, but didn't he give any reason for ringing me?'

'No — just for you to call back as soon as you possibly could. I'll get off the line so that you can do just that. Glad I caught you,' she repeated. 'Bye.'

'Goodbye, Chloe.' Belatedly she added, 'And — thanks.' But Chloe had already hung up.

Eve turned round slowly to face Bill, whose

frown of bewilderment matched her own. 'Was that my daughter?' he asked. 'Didn't she want to speak to me?'

Vaguely Eve registered that this was about the first time he had referred to Chloe in such formal tones; it effectively distanced them. She shook her head. 'I don't think she knew you were here. She rang to tell me there was an urgent message for me on your answering machine — from England. I must get in touch at once.' She looked round for the telephone directory and began fumbling through the pages at the front.

'You won't find English numbers in there,' Bill told her in a dry voice. 'Anyway, if it is your family calling, you must know the number, surely?'

Eve threw him a quelling look. 'I am looking for the numbers to dial to get me out of Australia and into England,' she retorted through tight lips. If only, she thought, there were magic numbers that would do that quite literally for her. 'Ah — here they are.' With the forefinger of her left hand firmly keeping the place, she punched out the necessary numbers with her right hand, followed by her daughter's number.

Her daughter answered. Sobbing hysterically, she screamed into the phone, 'It's Dad — he — he — he's dead!' The last word ended on such a screech that Eve automatically moved the phone a distance from her ear. For one moment she stood there, icy cool. So, she thought, the bastard is dead. She couldn't see what it had to do with her, then Hugh came on the phone.

'You heard what Marion said.' It was a bald statement — not a question. 'Her father is dead. She is beside herself. I think you should come home. After all, he was your husband.'

'Ex-husband.' Eve cut in quickly with a heavy emphasis on the ex.

'Yes — well — your ex-husband. But Marion is your daughter and she needs you at a time like this.'

'Then it is about the first time since she was out of nappies,' Eve retorted, 'and anyway, what is wrong with you? Can't you look after her?'

'I — I . . . ' Hugh spluttered. 'I — well, I don't seem much good at this sort of thing. I feel it is a mother's place to be with her daughter at a time like this.'

'You do?' Eve sighed, feeling, as she had done for most of her life, that the men she knew were hell-bent on railroading her into something she didn't want to do. Maybe in this instance he was right. After all, it would only mean going home a bit earlier since the events of the last half-hour or so had, it seemed, changed both her plans and Bill's opinion of her. She sighed. 'I'll see about a flight and let you know. Give my love to Marion,' She added as an afterthought.

Slowly she replaced the phone and turned to face Bill. He was staring at her, his face unsmiling. She willed him to say something — beg her not to go, give her an excuse to stay. Instead he said in a toneless voice that matched the expression on his face, 'Well, there you are, the perfect excuse to leave with dignity, *without losing face*, as the Chinese would say.' He shrugged. 'Would you like any help packing, making arrangements for someone else to look after the cat, getting you a flight, or would you prefer me to be on my way and leave you to it?' He looked down at the towelling robe he was still wearing, as if surprised to find he was not dressed. 'In the meantime I'll get my clothes on while you think about it.'

Mention of clothes reminded Eve that he wasn't the only one not dressed. 'I'll get dressed too,' she murmured and headed for the bedroom, quite forgetting that Bill's clothes were also there. He did not follow her and, feeling guilty that she had stopped him dressing, Eve began to scramble into her clothes as quickly as she could.

'If you chuck my clothes out I'll dress in

the bathroom,' Bill called. Quickly she complied, thinking all this was rather absurd considering they had spent the night together in the closest possible intimacy, when clothes had not only been unimportant but a nuisance.

Bill's thoughts ran along much the same lines as he collected his scattered garments — for Eve had taken him very literally at his word and thrown his clothes out of the bedroom door. Both of them were secretly wondering how something that had seemed so good between them could possibly disintegrate into this.

They reappeared in the kitchen simultaneously, decently and fully clothed.

'Well?' Bill sounded truculent. 'Have you decided whether or not I can be of any help, although no doubt Alex would be more than willing . . . '

Something snapped inside Eve. Why was she walking on eggshells in her dealing with Bill? The lovely dream was over — finished. He had made it clear he didn't want or need her, even trust her. In a short time she would leave Australia for good to go back where she was at least needed. She thought of her spoilt, selfish daughter and pompous, self-righteous son-in-law and indignation welled within her at the peremptory way they were summoning her — and for what? Because her divorced husband had died. His total selfishness and constant nitpicking had killed any feeling she ever had for him long before the divorce, so why on earth should she rush back now?

On a deep breath, she faced Bill. 'I have no intention of rushing back to England,' she told him. 'So as I don't need any help with anything — anything at all — there is no need whatsoever for you to stay.' She stared at him, still breathing fast. Where had so much defiance came from? 'But thanks for the offer, all the same.'

Now he was being dismissed, leaving was the last thing Bill wanted to do. As they stared belligerently at each other, the idea of compromise flitted into each of their minds. While Eve was still searching for words to ask him to stay without actually grovelling, Bill said with assumed nonchalance, 'I would like to go to England myself. If you could wait a while, maybe we could — well — travel together?'

'Maybe we could.' Eve was non-committal but a small smile began to play round the corners of her mouth. They stared at one another then as if of their own volition, their feet moved towards each other and Eve found herself in his arms, laughing up into his face.

'That wouldn't be a proposal, would it?' she asked.

'No — just the precursor to one. Will you stay here and marry me — in real time, not cyber space?'

Eve nodded. 'I'll certainly give it consideration — but bear in mind I am not the same meek little mouse who came out here. From now on I refuse to be ordered around by any male chauvinist.'

'Don't worry — we will get along just fine, so long as you remember the golden rule . . .'

'Which is?'

'Add a pinch of sugar to everything you say to me — but take everything I say with a grain of salt.'

Eve thought there was more than a hint of male chauvinism about that; she was about to tell him so in her new-found rebellion against the dominance of the male, but it just might be smarter to let him think she totally agreed. Then she caught the laughter in his eyes and knew that they would work their marriage out in their own unique way and surrendered herself to his kiss.

J